DOC

SILVER SAINTS MC

FIONA DAVENPORT

DOC

SILVER SAINTS MC

Oakley Collins thought her internship with a county judge was her ticket to getting into a great law school. Instead, it got her talked onto the back of Kendrick "Doc" Lawson's bike when she was in the wrong place at the wrong time.

As the Silver Saints' fixer, Doc had a reputation for keeping calm in any situation. Until he stumbled across the beautiful college student while breaking into the judge's chambers, looking for proof that he was crooked. Then his mission took a backseat to keeping the woman he planned to claim safe.

1

DOC

"Sit," Jared "Mac" Mackenzie growled as he dropped down onto the big leather chair behind his desk. The president of my MC—the Silver Saints—had called me in for a meeting after dinner.

I sat on the overstuffed couch on the wall next to the door and stretched my legs out, resting them on the coffee table and crossing my ankles. Our VP, Scout, stood next to the prez, leaning his hip on the desk.

"Got a call from Gary Finch," Scout informed me.

My lips pressed together, and I swallowed a grunt of disgust. Gary Finch was a slimy, unethical lawyer who would serve any master if the ante was high enough. I would've been more than happy to slit the asshole's throat, but he was a necessary evil.

The only honest lawyer willing to work with the MC was on hiatus. Jasper and his wife were in China wading through red tape to adopt a six-year-old boy and his three-year-old sister. There was no telling when they'd be back.

Jasper was a straight arrow, but he saw our complete loyalty to our brothers, how we treated our women, and the respect we had for anyone...until they'd earned our wrath. And he believed in our mission when it came to protecting people, making the scum of the earth disappear, staying away from drugs. So he turned a blind eye to our methods sometimes, along with all the other shit we had our hands in.

However, since he was an honest man, sometimes we were forced to work with fuckers like Gary.

"Rom got picked up two nights ago. Was in Devil's Jesters territory."

My jaw hardened at the name of the rival MC. They were known for their mistreatment of their women and being into shady shit. They also had it out for the Silver Saints ever since Patriot stole—and married—the sister-in-law of one of their citizens.

"Tell me another brother didn't snatch one of their women," I growled.

Patriot had saved Erin from being forced to submit to being a Devil's Jesters' old lady or a club bunny. According to him, he'd known she was his from the moment he saw her. I didn't understand it, but I respected his decision. However, making this shit a habit would put us at war, something we'd barely escaped with Patriot's situation.

"Naw," Scout answered with a shake of his head. "He was at a diner dropping off a package to a friend who lives in their territory. Police showed up because of a "tip" that he was carrying a stolen weapon. Since he didn't even have his own registered gun, he gave them permission to search his bike. Found the stolen pistol in one of his saddlebags."

I snorted. "They really thought he'd just carry it like that, so anyone could find it? Bullshit."

"Obviously planted," Mac muttered. "Cops in that territory are terrified of the club members, so they took him in."

"Security cameras?" This was always one of the first questions I asked when Mac called me in to give me an order. I was the club's fixer. The man who made problems disappear, whether by simply resolving the issue or taking care of business by any means necessary—as long as it was under the radar.

"That's one of the reasons Gary called. Seems the tapes that covered any angle of his bike were erased."

"Tapes?" I crossed my arms over my chest and leaned back in my chair. Most people used digital recordings these days.

"Yup," Mac said as he wrote something on a piece of paper, then handed it to me. "Lucky for us, that town is behind the times."

I nodded and took the slip of paper that had an address written on it. "I'll get copies and see what Hack can do with them." He was our resident hacker —one of the best in the world. If anyone could get something off those tapes, he could. "What was the other reason?"

Scout blew out a breath and pushed off the desk to pace. "Somehow, the judge fast-tracked the arraignment and skipped the bail hearing. No clue how he got around it, but Gary barely made it to the courthouse in time since they only contacted him an hour before the hearing yesterday morning."

"What the fuck?" I snarled. "Why are we just hearing about this now?"

"Cops swear up and down that he refused his phone call."

My mood darkened, and anger burned in my belly. I wasn't a sunshine and rainbows type of guy. The girls in the club often called me grumpy. Since it was a pretty accurate description, I just shrugged it off. But the only people who'd seen the truly dark side of me were my brothers. The Silver Saints weren't Boy Scouts. We lived by our own law, but injustice was something I'd never been able to tolerate—even if it was abusing the criminal justice system.

I wasn't a tortured soul or anything pussy-ish like that. My childhood had been normal and even a bit boring. But I'd seen enough of the underbelly of the world to be more than a little jaded. Plus, I'd always been a man of few words. It was one of the reasons I'd stopped including a woman in my thoughts about the future. Even if one had actually piqued my interest—which hadn't happened for a long fucking time—I wasn't the type to say sweet things and make love to a woman. And what were the chances I'd be as lucky as my brothers and meet a woman who would accept my lifestyle and how fucking dirty my hands were?

"Judge gave the lawyers less than twenty-four

hours for discovery, so Gary was scrambling, which was why he only just contacted us," Scout explained acidly. He obviously thought Gary's excuse was bullshit, and I had no doubt Scout would rough him up a little to make sure it didn't happen again.

"When is the preliminary hearing?" I asked, wondering how much time I had to get this mess untangled before it went to trial.

Mac slammed a fist on the desktop and shared a look with his VP before facing me once more, his eyes filled with rage. "He produced a document with Rom's signature that waived his right to the hearing."

"And he told the lawyers during a sidebar that if this proceeded to trial, Rom would most likely end up with the max prison time," Scout spat.

"Are you fucking kidding me?" I practically shouted. "It's his first offense of any kind. Rom's never had even so much as a speeding ticket. I don't give a fuck if the weapon was reported stolen. It's a misdemeanor at best."

"I agree, but the judge escalated it to a felony. Suggested a bullshit plea bargain of nine years," Scout informed me, his expression twisted with disgust. Which I completely understood since the max sentence for this crime was ten years in prison.

My hands balled into fists, making my knuckles

crack. "Let me guess, he also had proof that Rom confessed."

Mac nodded. "Yup, it's supposedly why he denied him bail."

I shook my head in disbelief. "This can't all be the Devil's Jesters. They don't have this much pull."

Running a hand over his beard, Mac grunted in frustration. "Gary thinks the judge is on the take."

Scout rolled his eyes. "He'd know all about that."

Yeah, Gary wasn't loyal to us for any other reason than we paid him a fuck ton of money for it.

Scout handed me another paper, this one with all the information they had on the crooked judge.

"Trial?" I asked.

"Next fucking week," Mac growled. "Don't know who this motherfucker is banging to be able to skirt the rules, but we need to find out."

"You need me to find proof that he's taking bribes?" I clarified. "And that the documents were forged?"

"And prove Rom's innocence," Mac added.

"Done."

2

OAKLEY

Pulling the throw blanket over my lap, I adjusted my glasses and aimed the remote control at my television as I settled into the corner of my couch. Then I stretched my legs out on the cushions next to me and scrolled through the options on my favorite streaming service. Snowball, my Persian cat, curled up on my lap with a purr.

As a sophomore in college, I should have more exciting things to do on a Friday night than watch shows with my cat. I'd overheard a couple of girls in my ethics class talking about a big party at one of the frats, but that definitely wasn't my kind of thing. Neither was hanging out in a bar, which I couldn't even get into since I wasn't old enough and didn't have a fake ID. Since I was already a week ahead on my homework, I didn't need to hang out at the library like usual.

Instead, I planned to catch up on a few of the newly released shows I had missed out on because I'd been too busy studying for a couple of exams over the past two weeks. Now that they were done—and I had aced them—I was looking forward to getting a little rest and relaxation this weekend.

After selecting a reality dating show about people who fall in love and get engaged before they actually see each other, I set the remote control on the side table. I was hoping the third season was as entertaining as the two that had come before it and planned to devour all twelve episodes before tomorrow night, even though it would take a dozen hours.

I grabbed the big bowl of popcorn I'd made and placed it next to Snowball. He flicked his tail in annoyance, so I stroked his back with one hand while I plucked a few buttery kernels with the other. Settling in to watch the first episode, I was quickly pulled into the newest season. I was trying to figure out who all was going to pair up when my cell phone vibrated.

Although I wasn't expecting anyone to call—my mom touched base with me on Sunday mornings—I had silenced my ringer so I wasn't bothered by any other notifications. My curiosity got the better of me. I brushed my bangs out of my face and pushed my glasses up my nose, then glanced over at the screen, quickly wishing that I hadn't.

If it had been anyone other than my direct advisor for my internship calling, I could have ignored my phone. Instead, I paused the show just as it was starting to get good and answered. "Hello."

"Oakley? It's Miss Stuchy."

"Yes?"

Her voice was impatient as she said, "I need you to go into the office and make three copies of the Tinley file."

"Now?"

"Yes, now," she snapped.

My brows drew together as I lifted my bowl of popcorn off my lap to set it back on the table. Having worked with Victoria—who insisted I call her Miss Stuchy even though we'd been working together ever since I started my internship two months ago—I knew she wasn't the kind of person who accepted excuses for anything. Even reasonable ones. "Does it have to be tonight? It'll be easier for me to pop into the office in the morning."

"Do you think I would've wasted time on my

Friday night calling you if it wasn't necessary for this to be taken care of right away?"

I barely held back my retort about how she didn't seem to have any issue with me missing out on my Friday night. I didn't have any hot plans besides watching television with my cat, but she had no way of knowing that I didn't have a life outside of school and my internship.

"No, probably not."

"Definitely not," she corrected. "Judge Timkins needs those copies first thing tomorrow morning, and I can't trust that you'll get this done in time unless you go in right now."

Her explanation didn't make any sense. Court wasn't open during the weekend, and the judge normally cut out early on Fridays. When I'd gotten the internship, I had been excited at the opportunity to learn from someone who had snagged a seat on the bench. I was studying pre-law with the hope to get into a prestigious law school after graduation.

At least the internship looked good on paper. It would still increase my odds of landing a clerkship once I reached that point in my education, which meant I couldn't risk getting fired. That wouldn't only blow my shot at a clerkship...it could ruin my chances of attending a decent law school. I couldn't let that happen when all of my future plans hinged on it.

"How will I get into the office?" I asked. "The courthouse is closed until Monday morning."

"Just because the courthouse is closed doesn't mean it's empty. There's still a security guard on duty. I'll call and ask him to let you inside so he's expecting you. Don't dawdle."

"I'll head over right away," I assured her. "Should I let you know when it's done?"

"And interrupt my Friday night even more?" she scoffed. "Absolutely not."

"Alrighty then," I mumbled when she ended the call without saying goodbye or thanking me for running this errand outside of the hours I was assigned to work. Although I was the lowest person on the office hierarchy, mine was an unpaid internship. The least she could've done was call someone who would earn time and a half for going into the office on a Friday night.

I shifted Snowball off my lap to set him on the floor, and he let out a plaintive meow. "Sorry, buddy. It looks as though Mommy has to go to work for a little bit."

Getting to my feet, I padded over to my closet and switched out of my cozy pajamas and into a slightly less comfortable outfit of black leggings with a black sweatshirt pulled over a gray T-shirt. Then I dumped the unpopped kernels out of the bowl and rinsed the butter and salt out of the bottom. Once that was done, I shoved my feet into my shoes and grabbed a bottle of water.

As I gathered my purse and keys, Snowball wound around my legs with a meow. Bending over, I picked him up to cradle his furry body against my chest. I gave him a scratch behind his ear and headed into the kitchen to grab his favorite treats. Pouring a couple into my palm, I moved my hand under his mouth so he could nibble on them. "There you go. Don't be too mad at me. I wish I was still cuddled up with you on the couch, too."

I walked over and dropped him onto a cushion, giving him another scratch.

"Keep my spot warm for me, Snowball." I kissed his nose, laughing softly at his grumpy expression. "Hopefully, this won't take too long, and we can get back to our binge-watching soon."

3

DOC

Working alone was always easier for me. No witnesses to keep quiet, no partners that could potentially betray you, no one to watch like a hawk so they don't screw up the whole fucking plan. The only people I trusted to help me were my brothers, and even then, only a select few. Although it was rare that I took anyone with me, they usually supported me from somewhere else. Like Hack's security company.

Entering the courthouse when it was open gave me the opportunity to blend in with the crowds, but it made bypassing access control systems much more difficult. There were times when the invisibility of a crowd was necessary, but this mission required solitude.

I wanted to get in and out unnoticed in case I couldn't find proof that Judge Timkins was making side deals, profiting off giving people lighter or harsher sentences than their crimes warranted. If I left empty-handed, I didn't want the judge on alert that someone was digging around in his life.

Hack had already done a deep dive into his life. He found plenty of skeletons, but none of them were enough to get the judge's ass thrown in jail. Disbarred, probably. Divorced, definitely. But not jail.

So we figured the trail must be on paper, which was why I was at his office later on a Friday night. And on the plus side, if I found something, he couldn't report the break-in without them wanting to know what was stolen. Then he'd be up shit creek without a paddle.

We'd let him stew a little while we handled Rom's case, though. One of our fill-in tail gunners, Knight, was a bounty hunter and could track just about anyone. Babysitting the judge was below his skill level, but when it involved another patch, he wouldn't trust the job to just anyone else. He worked with a couple of other fugitive recovery agents, particularly a married couple who saved his ass a time or two. They'd been more than happy to help when they heard about the judge's dirty dealings. So they would watch Timkins when Knight was unavailable.

"Unlocked the southwest fire exit," Grey said into my earpiece, breaking into my thoughts. He was Hack's best hacker and a good friend, so I trusted his skill. Plus, he'd already proven himself many times when he was a prospect and then a patch.

Security at the courthouse was minimal on the weekends because most doors and windows were locked, as well as offices, courtrooms, and other spaces—many that had restricted access during the day, as well. And CCTV footage covered most of the building.

"Motion lights?"

"Some young punks threw rocks at the lights this afternoon and broke a few," Grey said with laughter in his voice. Then he sighed. "Some people's kids."

I rolled my eyes, but the corners of my lips tipped up—pretty much the equivalent of a grin for me.

"Cameras?" I asked as I walked along the wall. The windows started an inch or two higher than my six-foot height, so there was no need to crouch. If I had been forced to walk bent at an angle, it might have attracted the attention of anyone who looked in this direction. Not that many people spent time walking around the entire building, but the parking lot was at the rear, so depending on the spot they chose, they had a good view of where I was. But most people ignored their surroundings, especially dark areas.

"Still frame," Grey answered. "But I can only pause them for ten to fifteen seconds at a time or anyone watching the screens will see the hitch in the feed."

I crept up to the door he'd opened for me, glanced around to make sure I was alone, then pulled it open and stepped into the stairwell. The interior of the courthouse had cream walls with expensive artwork, and everything else was made of dark wood. In stark contrast to that, the fire exits were gray concrete from top to bottom, with the exception of dark-blue railings and bright-red fire hoses. Every little sound echoed loud and clear, so I was careful not to let my boots squeak on the floor.

"The cameras are only on the landings," Grey informed me. "So stop two steps from the top, and I'll tell you when."

I did as I was told as he guided me up to the third floor where the judge's chamber was located.

"The door to his office is about a thousand feet to

your left. There are two cameras that cover that area. Just a sec—okay go."

I slipped into the hallway and beat a silent path to Timkins' chambers. It was restricted by a keypad and a fingerprint scanner, but the biometrics in the building had broken down that morning...I hooked up the decoder and let it do its thing. In less than five seconds, the lock disengaged, and I was able to slip into the office, narrowly missing Grey's window on the cameras.

"I don't have eyes in there, so just let me know when you're ready to leave," Grey reminded me. Apparently, the judge was too "private," which meant paranoid in my book, to have cameras in his chambers. He relied solely on the controlled access and distress alarms.

Silently, I shut the door behind me and looked around. The chambers were a large suite of rooms, smaller offices, a conference room, a bathroom, and a few others. But I walked toward the one with the obnoxiously ornate knocker on it. The guy was a pompous ass, and it didn't surprise me one bit that he would make sure his space was distinct.

A delicious scent wafted to my nose, and my feet automatically moved toward it. There was a small, neat desk in one corner, and although I didn't see a candle or lotion or anything that would be producing the smell, it was strongest there. Breathing deeply, I felt my mouth water at the hints of vanilla and cinnamon in the air. And to my utter shock, my dick stirred. *What the fuck?*

"Everything okay?" Grey inquired, reminding me where I was and making me feel like a complete pussy for being captivated by a scent, especially such a feminine one. I'd been so distracted by it that I hadn't responded to his comment.

I cleared my throat, but my voice was gruff when I answered. "Yeah, just getting the lay of the land."

Forcing myself to walk away from the tantalizing aroma, I headed toward the big office. There was moonlight filtering through the tall windows, so I didn't need to use my flashlight to find my way around. However, when I entered the judge's room, I pulled it from my pocket to help me see smaller details. Like the labels on the file cabinets, and indications of hiding spots.

I opened the first file drawer and started combing the papers. When I didn't find anything damning, I moved to the next. It was unlikely that the guy would be stupid enough to leave evidence of his misdeeds in an easily accessible spot like that. However, sometimes hiding in plain sight was the safest bet...like fading into a crowd.

And who knew what other dirt I might find, so I went through the entire cabinet. I found plenty of case files where the defendants were completely screwed over in the justice process and even more who were given sentences that were outrageous in relation to the crime. In many cases, like Rom's, misdemeanors were escalated to felonies on a technicality. Then there were the opposite cases, ones where people who should have been sent to prison for life, or at least longer than five years, such as the drug kingpin whose file I was reading.

I replaced the cases, shaking my head in disgust. We needed to take this motherfucker down by any means necessary. Mac wouldn't agree, especially when the guy was so high profile, but I was a fucking fixer. I knew how to make it look like a suicide, or he'd overdosed with one of the druggies he'd let off with a light sentence. Hell, I could make it look like a fucking heart attack and no one—and I mean *no one* —would know the difference. I was that fucking good.

I finished up with the first cabinet, then decided to do a little creeping around before starting on the next one. Without disturbing much—slight shifting of items and the chair could be explained by custodial—I ran my hands over the desk, feeling for out of place notches, gaps in the seams, or anything that didn't feel right.

Just as my fingers were gliding over a bump in the floor beneath the desk—the bulge was distinctly different that the one that covered a distress alarm—Gray coughed in my ear.

"Shit. Fuck. Someone is headed your way."

"What?" I hissed, my temper spiking.

"She's young and dressed so casually, I assumed she would be heading to the records room or somewhere like that. But she got off on the third floor and turned toward Timkins' office."

The judge's suite and courtroom took up a good portion of the left wing on the third floor. "You sure she isn't headed somewhere else?"

"Yeah, brother. She's about to walk into the outer office. Better make yourself invisible until she gets whatever she came for. Probably just left her purse or whatever and will be gone in a minute."

Just in case, I took my gun out of the holster, then stepped into the shadows, close enough to be hidden but with some visibility of the unexpected visitor.

"I can't believe I'm here on a freaking Friday night," a sweet but irritated voice huffed adorably.

"Not that I had better plans, but she didn't know that. Okay, that was a little mean. Bingeing with Snowball is a great activity."

She didn't sound convinced, and it curled the corners of my mouth up.

The scent of cinnamon and vanilla suddenly got stronger, and I realized that the small desk out front must have been hers. Fuck, it was making me hungry.

After a second, she sighed, and I nearly stumbled backward when my dick jumped to life. Was that what she would sound like after being thoroughly satisfied in bed?

For fuck's sake! What are you thinking, Lawson?

Apparently, my cock was doing all the thinking. And it only got worse when the lights flipped on and the mystery woman came into view.

4

OAKLEY

I'd never been in the office when nobody else was around, and I quickly discovered that I wasn't a fan of being alone in the dark, empty space. When I flicked on the lights, some of my nerves settled but not all. The sooner I made those copies, the sooner I could leave. So I hurried over to my desk to drop my purse on the corner and pulled my chair out, swiveling it around toward me. As I dropped onto the seat, I glanced up. I had a direct view of the judge's office from my little spot in the corner.

I had been too irritated by the fact that I'd had to go all the way across town to the courthouse to notice that his door was open until I was staring right at it. Judge Timkins was a stickler about staff not invading his privacy, and he kept his door closed most of the time when he was working. One of the first rules I was given when I'd been assigned to his team was to use the ridiculous knocker to announce my presence and wait for the judge to give me permission to enter.

I couldn't recall a single time when he didn't lock that door before he left. "That's weird."

Padding across the room, I paused at the doorway. I was in a lose-lose situation and wasn't sure what the best course of action was.

If the judge found out that I went into his office when he wasn't there, I could lose my internship. But if he learned that the door was open and I didn't check to make sure everything was okay, then I could lose my internship. Either way, my future was at risk, so I figured I might as well assuage my curiosity.

After taking a few steps into the judge's office, I paused to scan the room. With only the moonlight coming through the windows, I couldn't see much, but nothing seemed out of place. I didn't hear anything, either. But I couldn't shake off the eerie feeling that I wasn't alone.

Huffing out a breath that ruffled my bangs, I muttered, "I really should've ignored Miss Stuchy's call. If I hadn't answered right away, she probably would've just moved on to the next person, and then I'd still be cuddled on the couch with Snowball."

I heard the slightest sound near the desk, and my head jerked in that direction. Squinting my eyes, I finally realized the large shadow I was staring at was actually the body of a man. At the realization that I wasn't alone, I pressed my trembling fingers against my lips.

The guy shouldn't have been able to hide so easily with how big he was. And he definitely shouldn't have been able to move so quickly, either. But before I had the chance to react, he was across the room, wrapping a hand around my biceps and placing the other over my mouth.

Now that he was close enough, I could see what he looked like. And oh my goodness, was he hot. With his thick, dark hair, short-trimmed beard and mustache, dark eyes, and big, muscular body covered in dark leather clothing, he was like a sexy spy but with rougher edges.

He stared at me intently, and somehow, I knew he was silently asking me not to scream. There must have been something seriously wrong with me because instead of yelling at the top of my lungs, I was eating him up with my eyes. It took a lot of effort to gather my scattered wits, but I nodded, and he hesitantly uncovered my mouth and took hold of my other arm.

"What are you doing in here? The judge's chambers are off-limits." I glanced over my shoulder at the room I'd come from. "And the building is closed. Did the security guard let you in? He didn't mention there was anyone else around when he let me in."

"I think the better question is what are you doing here?" His voice was low and gritty, sending tingles straight to my core.

My brows drew together as I rubbed the back of my neck. "Um, no. You can't just turn my question back around on me when that's what I asked you. No way am I answering until you give me a good reason not to scream for the security guard."

I should've already been calling for help, but I didn't get any threatening vibes from this guy. As someone who had spent her life being a wallflower, I had a lot of time to observe people. I was a fairly good judge of character, and I couldn't picture this guy hurting me, no matter how intimidating his size was, especially compared to mine.

"Shit," he hissed, his nostrils flaring. "I get why you'd want to scream, but if you do, I'm gonna wind up in prison...probably for a fuck of a lot longer than the law intends if Timkins has his way, judging by his track record."

I frowned up at him. "The judge would be angry

about you being in here, but that doesn't make any sense. He wouldn't be assigned to your case, and judges only have so much leeway. There are very strict guidelines for sentencing."

"Like a fucking lamb to the slaughter." His thumbs stroked over my arms, making me happy I'd thrown on a sweatshirt so he didn't see the goose bumps left in the wake of his touch. "You're too damn sweet to be working in a place like this if you don't realize that there's always a way to get around the rules when you have enough power."

"Is that how you got in here? Because you've got power, too?" I tilted my head to the side, a lock of my hair sliding over my shoulder and curling around his wrist. "Do you have something to do with why the security guard warned me that the biometric scanners are down, and I just needed to use my code to get into the office?"

"The only connections I have are my club brothers."

That wasn't really an answer either way, but it sparked more curiosity in me. "Club brothers?"

"I can't believe I'm doing this," he muttered as he unzipped his leather jacket to show me the vest beneath it. Releasing one of my arms, he tapped one of the patches over his broad chest. "I'm a Silver Saint."

I clearly needed to get out more often because he said it as though I should've known who the Silver Saints were when I'd never heard of them before. I didn't even know there were any motorcycle clubs in the area. The only reason I had any clue what that vest meant was because I'd seen MC cuts just like it on television.

Based on the storylines on those shows, I should've tried to run screaming from the room. But I read an article a month or two ago about how a motorcycle club had helped protect a little girl who'd been bullied at school after her dad died, and I couldn't help but wonder if the reason I wasn't getting a scary vibe from this guy was because he was one of the bikers who tried to make a difference. Considering he hadn't threatened to hurt me—or just gone ahead and done it—I figured the odds were good that my instinct about him was right.

"Here's the thing...I'm not sure why you're here, but if I don't make the copies that I was ordered to take care of, that will raise some questions I'm pretty sure you won't want me to answer. The guard put my name down in the log, so my supervisor will be able to easily confirm that I was here." I lifted my chin while pursing my lips. "And if I'm in here too long, the guard might come looking for me, which I'm guessing is the last thing you want to happen."

He scrubbed his hand over his beard. "Are you trying to protect me from getting caught?"

"Maybe?" I shrugged. "I've been accused of seeing the bright side of everything before, so I guess that could be what I'm doing now. But I figure if you haven't hurt me yet, then you're probably not going to."

"Hurt you?" His head jerked back. "Never."

There was no missing the outrage in his dark eyes. "Then I think I should make those copies so we can get out of here before the security guard shows up."

He stuck close as I completed the task Miss Stuchy had assigned me. Once it was done, he picked up my purse and turned toward me. "Did you drive yourself here?"

"Nope." I shook my head. "I don't have a car, so I took a rideshare."

"A fucking rideshare by yourself on a Friday night." The vein in his temple throbbed as he shook his head. "No way in hell is that happening again."

"Is that your subtle way of offering me a ride?" I asked as he shut the judge's door and scanned the outer office, probably checking to make sure every-thing looked the way it should so nobody would suspect that he'd been here.

He speared me with his dark gaze. "Are you gonna walk past that security guard without saying a word and meet me at my bike?"

"That depends...do you have a good reason for being here?" I toyed with the rim of my glasses, holding my breath while I waited for his answer.

He nodded. "Yeah, a damn good one."

"Then I guess you're my ride home." At his grimace, I tilted my head to the side and narrowed my eyes. "If not home, then where?"

"My clubhouse. Not sure it's safe for you to go home at the moment, and I'm sure you've got more questions for me."

Not only had he brought my dormant libido to life, he'd also piqued my curiosity. "We should intro-duce ourselves since it sounds as though we're going to be spending a little more time together. I'm Oakley Collins."

"You're too damn sweet for your own good, Oakley Collins." Before he zipped his leather jacket back up, he patted the other side of his vest. "I'm Kendrick Lawson, but everyone calls me Doc."

5

During the whole ride to the clubhouse, I kept coming up with reasons I should turn the fuck around and take this sweet thing home. What was I supposed to do with an innocent girl like her? *Other than fuck her*, I silently muttered to my aching cock.

I was jaded, an asshole most of the time, and when she found out what I did for a living, she would most likely run for the hills anyway.

But with her soft body pressed into the back of mine, her arms wrapped around my chest, and her thighs plastered to my legs...I came up with just as many reasons to keep her. She needed someone to protect her, especially being so trusting while working for scum like Timkins. Besides, I needed to make sure she kept her mouth shut...and there were plenty of ways to accomplish that.

Then there was the fact that she was the first woman to tempt me in the slightest in longer than I could remember. And I didn't just want her...I *craved* her. Even with the wind whipping around us, her smell filled my lungs, intensifying my hunger to taste her.

As the compound came into view, my thoughts shifted to the club. Prez would be so fucking pissed. I'd just kidnapped someone for a flimsy reason, even if she'd been willing to get on my bike because she didn't realize she wouldn't be leaving the clubhouse anytime soon. And taking her was bound to be a big deal since she worked for the judge. If it ever got out that she'd been taken by a Silver Saint, it could cost the club in reputation and revenue. I tried to focus on that, telling myself I'd just make sure she stayed quiet and then take her home. Mac would still be pissed, but he'd get over it.

Except...I already knew I wasn't going to give her up.

I slowed my bike as I neared the guard shack at the entrance. Cash was on duty, and he raised an eyebrow when he spotted my passenger. "Talked to Grey," he drawled as we came to a stop. I'd turned off my earpiece when I confronted Oakley, then only turned it back on to tell him I was out and on my way home. "Didn't mention that you took a hostage. Mac know you brought her here?"

I gave him a stony stare that was all the confirmation he needed. Then he opened his mouth with a spark in his eye that told me he was about to make some smart-ass remark that I would normally ignore, but in my current state, I'd probably slam my fist into his face.

"Don't," I growled.

He must have picked up on my mood, because he just smiled and gave us a jaunty salute before opening the gate. The drive to the clubhouse from the gate was only a few minutes, but by the time I parked in one of the spots out front, I'd stopped wavering, and came to a definite decision.

After kicking the stand down, I shut off the engine and pocketed the key in my leather pants. I'd given Oakley my jacket to wear and suppressed a smile at how adorable she looked swimming in it. Gently, I unbuckled the helmet on her head and lifted the visor so I could take her glasses off her face. Then I removed the helmet, letting all of her silky, dark brown hair fall around her shoulders, before brushing her bangs away and setting the spectacles back on her pert little nose.

I'd never considered glasses sexy, but on Oakley, they were hot as fuck. Everything about her was a turn-on. She was around a half a foot shorter than me, with a waiflike body shape that reminded me of a fairy. Her beauty was understated, so I imagined that not a lot of people recognized how absolutely drop-dead gorgeous she was. Which was fine with me. I didn't think she'd appreciate it if I was constantly gouging out the eyes of men who looked at her a little too long.

Oakley was quiet as I helped her off the bike, her deep brown eyes studying me as if I were a puzzle she hadn't yet worked out. I knew she was curious about what was going on, but she waited patiently rather than pestering me about it.

"Let's go inside, and we can talk."

"Okay." I put my hand at the small of her back and urged her toward the front door. It gave me a stellar view of her legs and ass in the legging-things she was wearing. I would definitely have to put my foot down on her wearing those anywhere but our bedroom, and eventually, our house.

My dick was painfully hard, so I peeled my eyes off her assets as we walked up to the door. She turned slightly, glancing around, and something in her expression and the sharp intelligence in her eyes told me that she didn't miss much.

"This place is impressive," she told me quietly. "It's nothing like I pictured for a motorcycle club."

I nodded and urged her to step inside with a little pressure at her back. "Depending on where you got your information, it was most likely inaccurate or based on clubs that are very different from the Silver Saints."

"So it would seem," she replied as she took in the large front room on her right, with couches, tables, and a bar. The wall on our left was covered with photos from races and events dating from this year to back to when the club was founded.

A few of my brothers were lounging around, and a couple of old ladies were sitting at the bar with Cat standing behind it. Everyone's eyes were on us, and I glared at them as I slipped my arm around Oakley, pulling her against my side.

I was a little surprised when she melted into me, but I took it as a sign that she was feeling this thing between us as much as I was.

Heavy footfalls came from down a hallway a few feet ahead of us, and I braced myself when the prez stomped around the corner. He scanned the room, then his eyes landed on me, and I gulped at the fury in them. I was not easily intimidated, but Mac was president of the club for many reasons, including being a scary motherfucker who didn't take shit from anyone. He was softer with the women and children, and he ruled with fairness, but he didn't tolerate being disobeyed, and he wouldn't hesitate to punish a brother with a bullet between the eyes if they disrespected the club.

Lucky for me—*sort of*—he hadn't given me an order not to snatch Oakley and bring her to the compound. However, his rage was still justifiable because the repercussions could be really bad. Still, I wasn't going to give her up, and if that meant handing over my cut and patch, then so be it.

Mac pointed at me. "You. Office." Then he looked at the bar and used three fingers to beckon Cat over. Although he gave her an order, his voice was slightly gentler. "Take—" He frowned and looked at me.

"Oakley."

"Take Oakley to the kitchen and feed her. Then you can put her in—"

"She'll stay with me," I interrupted firmly.

Mac's eyes narrowed, practically burning through me when he growled, "We'll discuss it."

"I want to stay with Doc," Oakley piped up.

I pressed my hand over her mouth and nodded out of respect for my president, but I knew he could see by the stubborn expression on my face that I wasn't going to budge.

After staring me down for a few seconds, he growled and turned back to Cat. "After she eats, you can put her in Doc's room. *For now.*" He stressed the last two words with a meaningful glance at me.

Cat murmured her agreement and smiled warmly at Oakley. She jerked her head toward the other side of the room where the entrance to the kitchen was. "Come on, kid."

Oakley's eyes raised to mine, not with fear, but more like she was making sure it was okay for her to leave. I wanted to laugh because it was adorable that she thought she could protect me. Especially when I already knew that she had the ability to shatter my heart.

"Maybe I shouldn't leave you with—"

Cutting her off, I curled my arm in and brought Oakley around so her front was plastered to mine. Then I plunged my free hand into the back of her hair and fisted the soft strands, holding her head at just the right angle. My lips sealed over hers, and I was bombarded by a torrent of sensations I hadn't been ready for.

My tongue traced the seam of her lips, and they parted for me. I groaned when her cinnamon and vanilla taste burst in my mouth. I couldn't think of anything except...more. I wanted to feel her heated skin sliding against mine, taste her pussy to see if it was as sweet as her mouth, feel her tight channel squeezing the fuck out of my cock.

I was seconds away from sweeping her into my arms and marching into my room when our moment was smashed to bits.

"Doc!" Mac snapped. "Get your ass in my office before I rip off your balls and assign you to pick up every bullet casing in the woods behind the range. Then I'll decide whether or not to make you swallow one."

Oakley gasped. "That was rude," she muttered. I swallowed my laughter because Mac looked like he wasn't sure whether to strangle her or burst out laughing as well.

Instead, I turned a gentle smile her way. I couldn't tell her Mac was kidding because he would absolutely do what he said. So I just kissed the tip of her nose and gave her a soft pat on the ass. "Go with Cat, baby. I'll see you in a bit. And don't wander alone." I grabbed her chin and stared into her eyes so she understood I was serious. "Do not ever roam around the clubhouse unescorted by me, Cat, or one of the other old ladies. Is that clear?"

"Okay," she agreed with a pout. I kissed her hard and fast, then handed her off to Cat.

Mac didn't wait for me to make sure Oakley was all right. He grabbed the back of my cut and hauled me down the hallway to his office.

Picking my battles, I didn't fight him. When we were inside, he let me go and stomped around his desk to drop onto his chair.

"Shut the door and then explain to me what the fuck you were thinking by kidnapping a girl and bringing her to the compound."

I kicked it shut and took a seat in one of the chairs in front of the large, wooden desk.

Quickly, I gave him a run down of the entire evening.

"Do you realize the shitstorm you may have brought down on the club, Lawson?" Calling me by my last name rather than my road name was not a good sign. "You kidnapped the intern of a county judge. At best, he'll just be tipped off that someone is fucking with him. Worst case, someone finds out it was you, and not only will the mob be coming after you, you'll tarnish our reputation."

"Didn't you kidnap your old lady?" I asked nonchalantly, willing to tug on any thread that might bring him around to see my side of things.

"That's different," he gruffed. "She came willingly, and I did it in retaliation for a crime committed against the club."

"You don't consider what Timkins did to Rom a crime against the club?"

Mac mulled that over for a minute, and I was pretty sure I was making some progress toward keeping my balls and patch.

"I didn't force Oakley onto my bike."

Mac considered that, but he wasn't completely convinced.

"Bridget was mine."

"Exactly."

His brow rose, and he studied me carefully. "You're claiming her?"

"Fuck yeah, I am."

Watching me carefully, he rubbed a hand over his salt-and-pepper beard, then sighed. "What are you going to do with her?"

"Keep her."

Mac snorted. "Good luck with that."

I grinned. Oakley definitely had a feisty side, but from the way she reacted to my touch, I didn't think I'd have any problem convincing her to stay with me. After enough orgasms, she'd eventually fall for me, too. A thought popped in my head, and I was surprised that it didn't freak me out.

Knocking her up would certainly help convince her to say.

6

OAKLEY

I was in a daze from Doc's kiss as I followed Cat into the kitchen. It wasn't until she had me seated at a long table and was asking me what I wanted to eat that I realized how out of it I was. "Um, I'm actually not hungry. I already had dinner and a big bowl of popcorn tonight."

She quirked a brow. "Being kidnapped didn't work up an appetite for you?"

"Kidnapped?" I echoed softly, remembering what the guy who'd let us past the gate had said. "Why does everyone think that? Doc just brought me back here because he didn't like the idea of me taking a rideshare and wasn't sure it was safe for him to take me straight to my place. I'm sure once he's done with his talk with that guy who seemed really angry with him, we'll talk about what he was doing at the judge's office and then he'll take me home."

I sounded as disappointed by the last part as I felt, which Cat didn't miss. "You really think you're going home anytime soon?"

Nodding, I strummed my fingers against the top of the table. "Yeah."

"Even with how Doc just laid that kiss on you, insisted you stay in his room, and growled at you about never wandering around the clubhouse alone?"

She had me there because it certainly seemed as though he was expecting me to be around longer than I'd anticipated when I got on the back of his motorcycle. "I...ah..."

"You strike me as a really sweet girl, so I hate to be the one to tell you this...but you're the most willing kidnapping victim I've seen around here since Mac took Bridget. And she provided the ladder they used to climb out her bedroom window."

My eyes widened in shock. "One of the Silver Saints kidnapped a woman? And she helped him do it?"

"Remember that guy who was so angry with Doc?" she asked with a grin.

I nodded. "Uh-huh."

"That was Mac, the president of the Silver Saints MC."

"Oh." I twisted around to look through the doorway behind me as I muttered, "I knew I shouldn't have let Doc go for that chat by himself. Mac probably thinks he really did kidnap me."

"Because he did," she murmured, her smile widening.

I leaned back in my chair and aimed my own grin at her. "We'll just have to agree to disagree until Doc proves you wrong."

"This is gonna be fun." Cat rubbed her palms together. "I'm so glad I was here tonight so that I have a front-row view of all of this going down."

She seemed confident enough in what she thought was happening that I started having some doubts. "On the off chance that you're actually right, I'm going to have to do something about Snowball."

"Who's Snowball?" she asked, dropping onto the chair across from me.

"My cat." I tugged my cell phone out of my pocket and pulled up a photo of my little fluff ball. "He's kind of spoiled and won't be happy if I'm not home at some point tonight to give him a treat and cuddle with him in bed. He can be a bit of a grump when he doesn't get exactly what he wants."

"Why am I not surprised you have a grumpy but adorable cat?"

I traced my fingertip over the image of his sweet face on the screen. "He's really a sweetie once you get to know him."

"You're adorable. I'd bet just about anything my old man is going to call you something like Sunny or Sunshine." At my look of confusion, she explained, "He likes to hand out nicknames to all the Silver Saints' old ladies."

I tugged on a lock of my dark hair. "But I'm not a blonde."

And I wasn't a Silver Saints' old lady, no matter how much I liked the sound of it.

"Yeah, but you've got the sunniest personality of anyone I've ever met." She shook her head with a soft laugh. "Which cracks me up since Doc is one grumpy dude."

He was a little on the quiet side, and I'd only seen him smile once tonight, but Doc didn't strike me as a grump. "He was really nice to me."

"I'm sure he was," she snorted. "He wants to get into your panties. Bad."

"I—" I was about to protest, but then I realized how silly that would be after the way Doc had kissed me. "You might be right about that, but it makes your kidnapping theory less believable because it would lower his odds of...um...getting in...um..."

"Your panties," she finished for me with a laugh. "I can see how you'd think that, but you don't know the Silver Saints men like I do. Mac wasn't the only one who resorted to kidnapping his woman before he claimed her."

I shook my head with a sigh. "I guess I can kind of sort of understand why you're so excited about that front-row seat even though I still think you have it all wrong when it comes to Doc and me. He'll probably take me home as soon as he's had a chance to explain why he was in the judge's office tonight."

"I don't know who the judge is—"

"Judge Timkins. I'm interning in his office," I interrupted. "When I went in tonight to make some copies he needs first thing tomorrow morning, I kind of stumbled across Doc breaking and entering."

Cat waved off my explanation. "And I don't need to know. If it's something I need to worry about, Scout will loop me in. That's how it works with club business. Most of the time, us women don't know a whole lot because the guys like us not to worry too much when it's shit they're gonna handle without our help anyway. These men are seriously invested in making sure their women sleep easy and don't take shit from anyone."

"Yeah, but this is different since I'm directly involved."

She lifted a shoulder before resting her elbow against the tabletop and propping up her chin with her palm. "I can see how you'd think so, but you're setting yourself up for disappointment if you think Doc is going to see it the same way. That's just not how these guys operate."

I narrowed my eyes with a harumph. "Not even when it's the smart play?"

"Maybe then." She lifted her other hand and squeezed her thumb and forefinger close together so there was only a tiny gap between them. "But I gotta tell you that based on my years of experience, the odds of that happening are slim. Especially with Doc since he tends to be a man of few words under normal circumstances."

"Doc is clearly involved in something connected to the judge, and I've worked for him for a couple of months. I'm pretty sure he'll see the benefit of filling me in on what's going on."

She beamed a smile at me. "Keep up with that sunshiny attitude. It's sweet, and I bet Doc can't get enough of it."

My cheeks heated at the innuendo in her tone. "I don't know about that."

"Trust me, I've been around the block long enough to recognize the signs." Her expression turned serious. "And if you're open to a bit of advice, the best way you can help Doc with the situation with the judge is not to give him a hard time when he tells you that he wants you to stick around until it's all figured out."

Spending time with Doc wouldn't be a hardship, but it wasn't that simple. "Assuming Doc asks me to stay here—which I don't think is going to happen—and that I agree, what about Snowball? I can't just leave him at my place alone."

"With the way Doc looked at you, I have no doubt he'll arrange for someone to pick up your kitty," she assured me.

"Do you really think so?"

"Yup, his room isn't the biggest in the clubhouse, but there's plenty of space for your cat." She stood and gestured for me to do the same. "I should probably take you up there since you're not hungry and that's where Mac and Doc told me to put you."

Curious about what Doc's room looked like, I followed her out of the kitchen and up the stairs.

"There is one thing that does surprise me about

this whole thing," she murmured as she stopped at a room that I assumed was Doc's.

"What's that?"

"That Doc let you keep your cell." She jerked her chin toward my pocket where I'd tucked my phone. "I'm not going to take it away from you since he obviously trusted you enough not to do anything stupid with it, like tell someone where you are while you're waiting for him."

7

DOC

My conversation with Mac moved to what I'd learned before I grabbed Oakley and got the hell out of there. It wasn't much, but another reason taking Oakley had been a good idea was because she might know more than she realized.

"We need to find evidence of the bribe he took for Rom's case," he grunted. "If Hack can't get those security files recovered, we'll need it to make sure he can't send Rom to prison for the next decade."

"Could take another shot at his office," I mused, scratching my beard. "But it's possible he keeps the files and ledger at home. Shouldn't be too hard to search there. His wife certainly lives it up with the extra money he's bringing in. Goes to the spa a few days a week and spends hours shopping, so the house is empty for several hours most days."

Mac tapped his fingers on the desktop as he considered what I'd said. "Hit the house and see what you find. If it's a dead end, then we'll consider the judge's chambers again."

"Will do," I replied as I stood.

"Your woman could be useful—"

"Not a chance in hell," I growled, taking a menacing step toward his desk.

Mac grinned, and I knew he'd been messing with me, and I had taken the bait like a fucking sucker.

"Figured as much," he grunted with a rough chuckle. "Now get the fuck out of my office and deal with your woman."

I jerked my chin up in acknowledgment, then stalked out of the office to the front lounge, where the stairs to the upper level were located. I took them two at a time, eager to see Oakley and make sure she was okay.

Cat hadn't always been so welcoming, but she'd learned her lesson when she'd said the wrong thing to Mac's old lady back when Bridget first arrived at the club. I had no reason to think she'd go back to her old habits, but this was my woman, and I wasn't completely rational when it came to her.

When I reached the door to my room, it was quiet on the other side. My first thought was that Oakley had somehow got away. But she'd been too curious to take off without having her questions answered, so I told myself to chill the fuck out and opened the door.

I had a house on a couple of acres not far from the compound, and I'd been slowly fixing it up for the last few years. It was habitable now but still unfurnished. And it was just easier to stay at the clubhouse, so I had a permanent room here.

Inside was a king-size bed, a nightstand, dresser, couch, and a flat screen mounted on the wall. I'd also added a small bookshelf with a stash of novels. The room was decently sized, but I didn't have the seniority yet to snag a room with a private bath. Which meant Oakley and I needed to move ASAP because if any of my brothers accidentally saw her in any state other than completely covered, I'd lose my shit.

The idea of shopping for the house had always made me grimace. Then I opened the door and saw my sweet, innocent girl curled up on my couch reading the spy novel that had been on the little table beside the bed.

Maybe...I mentally grinned at my brilliant idea.

I'd just give Oakley my credit card and tell her to buy whatever she wanted. It was going to be her home too, so she might as well be the one to pick everything out.

Her head lifted, and she pushed her glasses up her nose as she smiled at me. "Hi."

I grunted in response because I was too fucking distracted by thoughts of seeing her in those cute glasses and nothing else.

"I wouldn't have pegged you for a reader," she commented in a teasing tone. "Especially these kinds of books." She gestured to the bookcase, indicating my mixed collection of action/adventure, science fiction, mysteries, thrillers, and some of the classics, like David Copperfield.

My lips curled up as I walked in and shut the door behind me. "And what does my taste in books tell you about me?"

Oakley chuckled, and her cheeks tinged with pink. "That you have a great imagination?"

I raised an eyebrow, and my smile turned salacious as I ran my eyes over her from head to toe. "You're right, baby. I have a very creative imagination."

When my gaze returned to her face, her skin was flushed bright red. Hunger flared inside me when I spotted the tendrils of desire in her pretty brown eyes.

"So, um..." She shifted on the couch, looking a little restless. I couldn't help wondering if it was because she was wet. I was dying to find out, but she continued talking, and I wanted to answer her questions and get that out of the way before I took her to bed.

"We should talk before it gets too late. Not that I have any plans for tomorrow, but I don't want you to have to take me home in the middle of the night."

I didn't confirm or deny her assumption that I would be taking her back to her old place. She'd figure it out when she was underneath me in bed.

"What do you want to talk about?" I asked instead.

"What were you doing breaking into Judge Timkins' chambers?"

There was a lot that I couldn't share with her, so I was glad she started with a question I could actually answer. "Trying to gather evidence that he's been taking bribes in return for certain sentences."

Oakley looked dubious when she replied, "I don't know...he has to follow the protocols and laws."

I sat down next to Oakley, but it didn't feel right, so I grasped her hips and lifted her sideways onto my lap. Then I brushed her bangs out of her face and smiled before dropping my hand to rest it on her thigh. "I love that you're so innocent and see sunshine in every dark corner. I hate to be the one to darken any part of it. However, you need to know...the judge is a very corrupt, very dangerous man. When someone knows the legal system as well as he does, they can find all the ways around it."

She bit her lip and folded her hands demurely in her lap—it was adorable. "How do you know this about him?" Her expression and tone implied that she believed me, and I wanted to kiss her for giving me a little more of her trust.

"I can't tell you that, baby. It's club business."

"Even though I'm directly involved?" she spouted indignantly.

"Directly?" I repeated with a laugh, then gentled my tone when she looked disgruntled. "That's a bit of a stretch, baby. You were in the wrong place, at the wrong time"—or right place at the right time, depending on how you looked at it—"and that's the only reason I've shared as much with you as I have. Under normal circumstances, you wouldn't know anything about this shit."

I expected her to argue, and I could tell she

didn't like my answer, but she just muttered, "Yeah, Cat said something along those lines."

Nodding, I absently rubbed little circles on her thigh with my thumb. "Her old man is our VP. She and the prez's old lady, Bridget, know better than anyone what 'club business' means."

"And they're kept out of the loop because their men want to protect them?" Her voice was soft.

"Yeah. Nothing comes before protecting our women. It's the way it works in an MC—ours, anyway."

Oakley smiled wistfully. "It's probably really nice to have someone who cares about you so much. I guess I could see why they'd be okay with this way of life."

"Good," I grunted. "You'll get used to it."

Oakley's mouth dropped open, and I used my index finger to close it. "Now, I have a few questions for you."

I jumped right into them so she didn't have time to dwell on what I'd said. This was happening fast, but I wasn't gonna slow it down. Apparently, love happened fast and hard for the Silver Saints because I'd seen this with a lot of my brothers.

For the next fifteen minutes, I asked Oakley anything I thought she might know that would be helpful, as long as it didn't give away too much. She didn't know a lot, but her knowledge of the judge's schedule would be very useful.

When Oakley yawned, I called a halt to the questioning. "It's late, baby. Let's get you to bed."

"Yeah, we should get going," she sighed as she attempted to stand.

I wrapped my fingers firmly around her waist and turned her toward me so she had no choice but to straddle my legs. "Go where?"

"I thought you were going to take me home?"

"Absolutely not," I scoffed.

Her delicate features clouded over with confusion and disappointment. "Okay. I can call a rideshare. I just thought...well, never mind."

"You are not taking a fucking rideshare, Oakley," I growled.

"Um...So you are taking me home?"

Slowly, I glided one of my hands from her thigh up and around her hip to palm one of her ass cheeks. Then I captured her chin with the other, forcing her to look into my eyes as I yanked her body closer to mine. "Is that really what you want?" I inquired silkily as I raised my hips so the large bulge in my leather pants pressed into the heat between her legs.

She sucked in a fast breath, then held it as she contemplated what to do next.

To give her a little more incentive, I leaned in and brushed my lips over hers, then groaned and crushed our mouths together. With a firm tug on her chin, I parted her lips and plunged my tongue between them. "You taste so fucking good," I groaned after thoroughly plundering her mouth. "I want to know if you taste this delicious everywhere."

Oakley moaned and pressed her chest against mine. I could feel the hard points of her nipples poking through her shirt, and it sent streaks of pleasure straight to my dick.

I released her face and dipped my hand into her leggings to cup her pussy. Her panties were fucking soaked, and my mouth watered. "Tell me, Oakley," I demanded with my lips next to her ear. "Do you really want me to take you home? Or do you want to stay so I can feast on your juicy pussy?"

She shivered, and her lips chased mine, but I refused to go any further without making her admit how much she wanted this.

"Tell me."

Oakley sat back a few inches and licked her lips as our eyes met. "I want to stay."

8

OAKLEY

I had never so much as kissed another man, but here I was offering up my virginity to Doc on a silver platter because my panties just about spontaneously combusted when he said he wanted to feast on me. The words slipped out of my mouth before I realized I would agree, but I didn't regret them. Especially not when he pressed me onto the mattress and crashed his mouth against mine again.

I'd never reacted to another man the way I did with Doc. Something magnetic drew me to him, almost as though we were two pieces of a whole meant to fit together. And when he kissed me...I had a feeling I could easily become addicted to how he made me feel. The glide of Doc's tongue against mine, the scrape of his beard against my skin, his minty taste overwhelming my senses...combined together, they packed a powerful punch that left me breathless.

Twining my arms around his neck, I lost myself in the kiss that quickly spiraled out of control. When Doc finally tore his lips from mine, I let out a little whimper of protest.

His deep chuckle sent a sensual shiver up my spine. "Don't worry, baby. Now that I have you right where I want you, I'm nowhere near done."

Tugging on the hem of my sweatshirt, he lifted it and the shirt underneath over my head. His heated gaze zeroed in on the white lacy bra covering my breasts. "So fucking gorgeous."

I stroked my hands up his broad chest. "You're not so bad yourself."

"I'll show you not so bad," he rasped, lowering his head to use his teeth to pull down the lace covering one of my tits and wrapped his lips around the pebbled peak.

Arching my back off the mattress, I threaded my fingers through his thick hair to press his mouth closer to my chest. "Holy moly, that feels amazing, Doc."

He let my nipple go with a pop, his gaze locking with mine. "Kendrick."

"Hmm?"

"When I have you under me like this, you use my name, baby," he demanded. "I'm Kendrick to you, not Doc."

"Kendrick, please," I pleaded, loving that he wanted me to have the man and not just the biker. And he was setting a rule that made it sound like he intended for this to happen again.

He gave me what I wanted, stripping my bra from my body before lowering his head again to suck the other nipple deep into his mouth. I felt each tug of his lips deep in my core, as though there was a direct line from my breasts.

Cupping the slightly rounded swells, he kissed down the valley between, the scrape of his beard against my sensitive skin making me sigh in pleasure. Then he kept going lower, and the sound turned into a gasp when he yanked my leggings and panties down my legs and tossed them over his shoulder. I was sprawled naked beneath him, and there was no mistaking the masculine appreciation in his dark gaze, which helped ease some of my vulnerability.

I had never been naked in front of a man before, so it was a little weird lying here without a stitch of clothing on while he was fully dressed. But it was also thrilling.

My arousal was nearly overwhelming. Every muscle in my body was coiled tight. "I feel..."

"How do you feel, baby?" Kendrick asked as he wedged his shoulders between my thighs, making my core ache even more.

I struggled to find the right words since this was an entirely new experience for me. "Like I'm on the verge of...of...flying apart, maybe?"

"Hold on tight." He circled his fingers around my wrist and pressed my palm against his shoulder. "Because I'm sure as fuck going to make you fly apart for me. More than once."

"Yes," I gasped as his hands glided up my stomach to cup the underside of my tits, which felt heavy while he kneaded the soft flesh.

"But I need to know so I can make sure you're ready to take me when the time comes"—his dark eyes burned into mine as he used his thumbs to spread my pussy lips—"did you save your cherry for me, baby?"

My cheeks heated as I whispered, "I saved everything for you, Kendrick."

"My sweet baby." Intense satisfaction blazed in his brown orbs before he shifted his gaze to my pussy. "You have no fucking clue how grateful I am to hear that, but I'm gonna do my best to show you."

That was all the warning I got before he devoured me. Dragging his tongue up my seam to circle my clit, he licked between my folds from bottom to top and straight back down again. Over and over as my hips bucked off the bed.

"You taste fucking amazing," he groaned before thrusting his stiffened tongue into my channel, his hands gripping my hips to keep me still while he made a meal of my pussy. He used his fingers to manipulate my clit, and when he pinched the sensitive bundle of nerves, my release rolled over me in waves.

"Kendrick, yes! Oh, yes!" Gripping the sheets in my fists, I was stunned by the intense pleasure he'd given me. And he didn't let up, eating me through my orgasm until the shudders stopped. He didn't stop there, though.

"You've gotta give me another before I can sink my cock in your tight pussy," he growled as he licked inside again. "But on my fingers this time."

With my inner walls clamping around his thick digit, he had to work for every inch he thrust inside my pussy. As I was adjusting to his invasion, he twisted his wrist and stroked the pad of his fingers against a spot deep inside me that had me seeing stars. "Please, please, please," I chanted.

I wasn't sure what I was asking for, but Kendrick knew exactly what I needed. Wrapping his lips around my clit, he flicked his tongue over the bundle of sensitive nerves while sinking his finger in and out of me, making sure he hit the same spot each time. It shouldn't have been possible, but my second orgasm was bigger than the first. My screams of pleasure echoed off the walls as I dug my fingers into his scalp and rode his face until I practically melted into the mattress.

Only then did he let up, pressing a kiss against my inner thigh before getting to his knees. My eyes greedily ate up every inch of skin he exposed as he undressed. After he shrugged out of his leather vest and tossed it onto the couch, he pulled his shirt over his head, revealing a tattoo of an ornate cross on the right side of his six-pack abs and a piercing through his left nipple. My fingers itched to trace the black ink, and I wanted to suck the silver hoop into my mouth and roll my tongue over the silver ball at the bottom.

I was just about to reach out to touch his tattoo when my gaze locked on the bulge in his leather pants as he undid the button and slid down the zipper. The huge, impossible-to-miss bulge.

Although my body was relaxed from the orgasms

he'd given me, I started to freak out over how big it was when he distracted me by saying, "Slight miscalculation on my part. I should've taken these damn things off before you made me so fucking hard that it feels as though the leather is going to strangle my cock."

I couldn't stop the soft giggle that bubbled from my lips. "We can't have that."

"We sure as fuck can't." I gasped as his dick sprang free from his pants, the purple head bouncing off his six-pack abs. "The only thing that's gonna strangle my cock tonight is your tight pussy."

My breath caught in my throat. "Um...I don't want to be the cliché virgin, but are you sure it's going to fit?"

"Like you were fucking made for me," he assured without missing a beat.

His confidence eased some of my concern, but I still tensed up when his naked body stretched out over mine and the tip of his dick notched at my entrance. "Do you trust me?"

I didn't know him that well, and we'd met under unusual circumstances, but I didn't hesitate to answer, "Yes."

"Thank you, baby." He lowered his head to capture my mouth in a deep kiss at the same time that he punched his hips forward in one powerful thrust. Swallowing my cry of surprise, he held still while the pain passed and the smallest tendrils of pleasure started to creep in.

When I wiggled my hips, I gasped, "Oh."

Lifting his head, he searched my expression and asked, "Ready for more?"

"Uh-huh."

"Wrap your legs around my waist," he ordered, gripping one of my knees to help me. Then he slowly withdrew before plunging back in, starting slow until I begged for more.

"Kendrick, please. I'm so close."

"Fuck, baby," he groaned, picking up the pace. "You're so fucking tight, but you fit me perfectly, just like I said you would. Can't wait to feel your pussy milking my cock."

Wedging his arm between us, he flicked my clit, and he didn't have to wait any longer because I went off like a rocket. "Yes! Kendrick, yes!"

"That's it, sweet baby. Give it to me." He slammed into me a few more times before burying his face in my neck and groaning my name. "Oakley. My sweet Oakley."

We were both panting for air as he rolled onto his back, taking me with him so I was sprawled on his broad chest. I cuddled against him while I caught my breath and was just about to drift to sleep when I realized I was the worst kitty mommy ever. It'd been hours since I left my place, and I was never out this late. "I can't believe I forgot to talk to you about Snowball."

Doc tugged on my hair to tilt my head back so I was staring up at him as he asked, "Snowball?"

"Yeah, he's my very spoiled cat who will not be happy about being left alone for so long. You wore me out, but I can't go to sleep until I know he's taken care of."

"Don't worry, baby." He brushed a kiss against my forehead. "I'll go take care of your pussycat now that I've taken care of your pussy."

The second I walked into Oakley's place, I was practically attacked by a white ball of fluff. He ran up my body, and when I automatically curled my arms under him to keep him from falling, he plopped down like a king on a throne. Then he purred at me, and I had a feeling it was a demand to pet him.

Oakley had mentioned that her Snowball was spoiled, and I'd been prepared for him to try to scratch the hell out of me. I certainly hadn't expected him to take a liking to me, so much so that when I tried to put him down, he raised his head and hissed before dropping it down again to relax.

"Okay, buddy," I grunted. "Let's get one thing

straight. You may have Oakley wrapped around your little paw, but this shit won't fly with me. Now, you're going to let me put you down so I can pack you up and grab some of your momma's stuff, then I'll take you to her."

Snowball blinked at me a few times as if he was trying to decide what to do next. I would swear in court that he nodded regally, giving me permission. Which was impossible.

"Now you're imagining things, Lawson," I muttered. This time, when I bent over to set him down, he jumped out of my arms and stretched before marching over to a soft bed and curling up in it.

Shaking my head at the ridiculous cat, I went about throwing all of his stuff into a box I'd brought with me. Then I cleared out Oakley's bathroom and grabbed as many of her clothes as I could to fill up two duffel bags. After taking those down to my truck, I returned to the apartment to get his highness.

Snowball was waiting by the door when I walked in and immediately scurried up my body, forcing me to cradle him or let him fall. "Sneaky little mother-fucker, aren't you?"

He looked at me with the same indignant expression I'd seen on Oakley's face earlier. Then I reminded myself that cats don't have expressions and wondered if I should have my head examined.

Carrying Snowball in one arm, I grabbed the bed he'd been lying in and walked out into the hall. I shut and locked the door, then made my way down to my truck and headed back to the compound. I'd been away from Oakley for nearly an hour, and I was already feeling anxious. I'd have to put a fucking tracker on her and nanny cams all over our home, or I'd never get anything done. I'd be too busy worrying about her all the time.

When I returned to the compound, I ignored the grins of the few brothers I happened upon when they saw the white fluff in my arms. I went straight to my room and found Oakley sleeping peacefully in my bed. She was on her stomach, with one arm flung out to her side and the other curled under her head. The sheet barely covered her delectable ass, and one of her long, shapely legs was uncovered and bent at the knee. She looked fucking edible. But I told myself to back off. She'd been a virgin, and I'd been pretty rough with her. She needed to rest.

I set Snowball's bed on the ground and placed him on it, then hurried back to my truck to bring in everything I'd packed. When I returned, Snowball was curled up against Oakley's side in the middle of the bed.

"Oh no, your majesty. This is not how this works," I growled. Quickly, I stripped, then picked up the cat and set him back on his bed. Climbing into mine, I turned Oakley so her back was to my front and wrapped myself around her.

I felt the soft thump when Snowball jumped onto the foot of the bed, and I raised my head to glare at him. He blinked at me a few times, then took one step toward us but stopped when I growled. After an intense stare down, he yielded to me as alpha and circled twice before curling up to sleep at the end of the bed.

Sighing, I considered kicking him off, but I had to give him something after the way he backed down, so I left him alone. It didn't take me long to fall asleep with my woman snuggled up against me. But sometime in the night, I woke up with her ass pressed against my long, thick cock that was throbbing with need and my hand between her legs.

"Fuck," I rasped when I realized my fingers were drenched in her arousal.

"Kendrick," she moaned and squeezed her thighs together.

Lifting my head, I whispered in her ear, "Are you sore, baby?"

She quickly shook her head, and her thighs clenched again, making me groan as I dipped two fingers into her slippery channel. "Just...just...I ache," she whimpered.

"I got you, baby," I growled as lust built up inside me. I started moving my digits in and out, intending to finger her to an orgasm and go back to sleep. But when she cried out as she fell over the edge, I lost all reason.

Hooking an arm around her top leg, I lifted it and thrust my bare rod deep into her pussy. Then I curled her leg back to drape over mine, leaving her wide open. My hips moved in a steady rhythm as I caressed her, plucked and twisted her nipples, and kissed any skin I could reach. But eventually, my climax approached, and knowing I could get her pregnant sent me into a frenzy. I slid my hand down to her pussy and pinched her clit, sending her into a spiraling orgasm that had her screaming my name as she convulsed in ecstasy.

I managed to wait until she was coming down from her high before I pulled out, flipped her onto her back, and set her legs on my shoulders. Then I slammed home with a shout of bliss. I went so deep that I bumped her cervix, and that was all it took to lose control.

Bellowing her name, I exploded inside her, releasing copious amounts of come. The hot seed splashing into her womb set off another orgasm in Oakley, and she cried out again as it crashed over her.

Afterward, I flipped us over so she was sprawled over my body, and I was still sheathed in her heat. As we fell asleep, I promised myself to let her rest. But sometime in the early morning, I woke up hard and buried in her pussy. It would have been impossible not to fuck her one more time.

After a few more hours of sleep, I woke up to an empty bed and frowned, but relaxed when I saw Oakley again curled up on the couch, wearing my T-shirt, and reading a book.

"Morning, baby," I murmured as I sat up. "How are you feeling? Are you sore?"

Her cheeks turned pink as she met my eyes, and I fought not to grin so I wouldn't embarrass her more. "Um, only a little." Then she smiled even as her face flushed, and she admitted, "It's a good kind of sore, though. More like I'm...um...stretched, which makes sense since..." She trailed off as she gestured to my cock, which was tenting the sheet with my morning wood.

I couldn't help the grin this time, and it made her blush even harder. "That's good, baby. You'll always be snug, but you'll stretch easier with time." My smile turned wicked. "And a lot of practice."

Climbing out of bed, I winked at her before yanking on my leather pants, not bothering to button them. "I'll be right back. Gotta hit the head."

Oakley frowned and ran her eyes over me. "Do any of the old ladies or club bunnies stay here?"

I laughed, pretty sure where she was headed, but wanting to make her come right out and say it. "Mac's never allowed club bunnies, but even if he had, they'd have been long gone the moment Bridget stepped foot onto the compound. But yeah, some of the girlfriends or old ladies stay here on and off."

"And you just go traipsing around undressed like that?"

"What if I do?"

Oakley huffed, and I bit my cheek so I wouldn't laugh again. "Well, well, you...um...you shouldn't!"

Finally giving in to my smile, I prowled over to my woman and bent over her, pressing my fists into the back of the couch on either side of her. "Are you jealous, baby?"

Oakley looked like she was going to protest, but then she sighed and dropped her eyes to her lap as she admitted, "Yes."

"Baby, look at me." When she didn't do as I'd demanded right away, I growled, "Oakley."

She raised her eyes to mine, and twin spots of pink bloomed on her cheeks.

"See you being possessive of me...it's hot as fuck."

Oakley's lips parted in surprise before she grinned. "Really?"

I dropped a lingering kiss on her lips before murmuring, "Oh yeah. If your tasty little pussy didn't need a rest, I'd show you just how much I like it when you get jealous."

She swallowed hard and started to say something, but I put a finger over her lips.

"No. Be good now," I admonished. After giving her another quick, hard kiss, I grabbed a shirt from the dresser and pulled it on as I walked out into the hall.

Scout was just leaving the room he stayed in when he wasn't at home. Seeing me, he turned back and shouted, "You owe me fifty bucks, kitty cat!"

Then he grinned at me. "Cat didn't think you'd be able to talk sunshine into your bed last night."

I started to roll my eyes, then frowned. "Sunshine?"

Scout shrugged. "Cat's idea. Said it was the perfect nickname for your woman, and she's never wrong."

"Don't you forget it!" Cat shouted from inside the room, making Scout grin even wider.

"Hear you're pussy-whipped these days too."

I growled, irritated at anyone talking about my woman and pussy in the same sentence. No one should be thinking about her that way except me. "Don't talk about Oakley like that."

It wouldn't have surprised me if the smile he was sporting had cracked his face open, it was so big. "I wasn't talking about Oakley."

To my complete and utter horror, my cheeks heated when I realized he was talking about Snowball. Someone who saw me last night must have told him. I shook my head and scowled to cover up the blush. "Whatever it takes to make my woman happy."

Scout's expression filled with respect. "Happy for you, brother. Gotta say, I wasn't sure you'd ever find a woman willing to put up with your grumpy ass."

I flipped him the bird and disappeared into the bathroom, ignoring his raucous laughter while I took care of business. After washing my hands and brushing my teeth, I went back to my room to find Oakley pacing, her expression thoughtful.

"I was thinking..."

"Wouldn't have guessed that," I drawled, winking when she tossed me a glare.

"Anyway, I know you can't tell me everything because it's club business. But if you could just tell me exactly what evidence you are looking for, I could—"

"No fucking way," I snapped.

"But I have access, and no one would notice me. So you wouldn't have to break in—"

"Not a fucking chance in hell, Oakley," I snarled as I stalked over to stand in front of her. I crossed my arms and looked down, a stance that would intimidate most people. But Oakley just looked up at me like I was annoying, which made me want to laugh and growl at the same time. "You are not going back to that office."

"I have to finish my internship to get into a good law school!" she cried, throwing her hands in the air.

"We'll figure something else out," I told her, not willing to budge.

"I just want to help," she sighed.

Cupping her face in my hands, I stared into her deep brown eyes, making sure she heard every one of my words. "I will not ever knowingly put my woman in danger. Especially not when she's pregnant."

10

OAKLEY

"I am not pregnant," I sputtered. "Which you darn well know since you took my virginity just last night."

"And I didn't use a condom," he reminded me, stroking his thumb across my cheek. "I filled you with so much of my come, I'd be shocked if I didn't already knock you up."

"Oh." My lips formed a perfect circle as the possible outcome of all the unprotected sex we'd had finally dawned on me. "Wow, yeah...I guess you could be right since I'm not on any kind of birth control."

One of his hands dropped down to cover my belly. "I figured you weren't, baby."

"And that doesn't worry you?" I peered up at

him and didn't see even the tiniest inkling of concern in his dark gaze. "Do you have a bunch of baby mamas running around with your children or something?"

His lips curved, reminding me of how he'd told me he liked when I got possessive over him. "I can't remember the last time I've been with anyone. It's been that damn long. But one thing I know beyond a shadow of a doubt is that I've never gone bare before last night. You're the only one, Oakley."

"That makes me feel better, but I'm still not sure what to do with the fact that you seem unbothered that you might've already gotten me pregnant when we've only known each other for a day. I still have to finish my bachelor's degree, then three years in law school." My stomach let out a loud growl as Snowball wound around our legs with a plaintive meow. "I think I need breakfast before I try to wrap my head around how quickly things are moving between us, and I definitely need to feed Snowball before he starts yowling the clubhouse down."

He jerked his chin toward the closet. "I put a bunch of your stuff in there. You can get dressed while I feed the fluff ball."

"He's kind of picky about his food." My nose

wrinkled. "I hope you grabbed the cans out of the cabinet, or he'll refuse to eat."

Kendrick brushed a quick kiss against my lips before turning me toward the closet with a pat on my butt. "Don't worry, baby. Snowball will be fine. I got everything he'll need."

Swinging open the door to his closet, I found two duffel bags overflowing with my stuff on the floor. "Everything and then some."

By the time I was dressed—after using the bathroom with Kendrick standing guard in front of the door—and ready to head downstairs, Snowball was curled up on the couch with a belly full of his favorite cat food. I gave him a quick scratch behind the ears and looked up at Kendrick with big eyes. "Would it be okay if I bring him down with us? Judging by how much of my stuff you grabbed, it looks as though I'll probably be here for more than just a day, so I'd like for Snowball to get the chance to check out some of the clubhouse."

"Definitely more than a day," he grunted with a nod before guiding me downstairs with his hand on my lower back while I cuddled Snowball against my chest. The delicious scent of breakfast—bacon, for sure—wafted toward us as we neared the kitchen, and my stomach growled again.

"I should have gotten you a snack last night since we worked up an appetite."

My cheeks heated as I recalled all the ways we'd done that. "And I should have taken Cat up on her offer of food when we were in the kitchen, even if I wasn't hungry yet."

"Shit, baby. Sorry, I didn't realize you hadn't gotten anything to eat last night." He pushed the door open and nudged me toward the table. "I would've come down and gotten you something before I got ready this morning."

"I had no idea Doc could be so sweet," Cat cooed from the stove. "Aw, Snowball is even more adorable in person."

"And he didn't make her keep the fluff ball in his room." The man standing next to her flashed us a grin over his shoulder. "I guess the grumpier they are, the harder they fall, kitty cat."

"Shut up, Scout," Kendrick growled, stomping over to the stack of plates at the end of the counter.

"Is that any way to treat your VP?" Scout asked, turning toward Kendrick and crossing his arms over his chest.

He would've been intimidating if it weren't for the obvious spark of humor in his eyes, letting me know he was having a lot of fun pushing Kendrick's buttons. Not that it worked. Kendrick ignored the verbal jab and started to pile a bunch of food onto the plate he grabbed—about half of the bacon piled on a paper-towel-lined plate, a few pancakes with a thick square of butter on top, and several scoops of eggs. After tucking a fork and knife into the hand that was holding the plate of food, he grabbed the container of syrup.

Another guy strode into the kitchen as Kendrick turned toward me. "Thanks, Doc. I would say that you shouldn't have, but I'm fucking starving."

Kendrick yanked the plate out of his reach. "Not for you, Grey."

"C'mon, man. I'm just trying to help you out. That pile of food is a lot, even for you," he teased with a grin.

"It's not just for me." Kendrick stomped toward me and set the plate, silverware, and syrup on the table. "Oakley is hungry."

"Not *that* hungry," I mumbled at the pile of food in front of me.

"You sure about that, baby?" I blushed at his question since we'd just talked about how I'd worked up my appetite with sex. Brushing my bangs away from my glasses, he explained, "I didn't know what you liked, so I got some of everything and figured we could share."

"Whoa, Doc is willingly sharing his food?" Grey turned to stare at me. "With a chick I didn't even see sitting there? So much for me being observant."

"Don't worry, I tend to blend into the background a lot." I cast a meaningful look at Kendrick, even though he'd seemed pretty set on me not helping them search the judge's office. "Which can be useful in certain situations since most people don't pay much attention to me."

"I don't see how that's possible when you're so fucking gorgeous," he muttered, dropping down on the chair next to me and sliding the full plate between us. They must have bonded last night because Snowball climbed off my lap and onto his.

"Neither can I," Grey agreed with a grin aimed my way. "I spotted you right away last night when you popped up on the courthouse security feed."

"Also not for you," Kendrick grunted, getting to his feet to shrug out of his vest. Then he dropped it over my shoulders and tugged my arms through the holes before sitting back down.

My eyes widened as I tilted my head to stare at him. I assumed that the television shows had gotten a lot wrong about motorcycle clubs since he hadn't acted like any of the bikers on them, but there was something universal on all of the shows—a biker's cut was sacred. If he put it on a woman, he was serious about her.

Then again, considering the fact that he was so blasé about the possibility of getting me pregnant when we'd only met last night, I probably shouldn't be so surprised by this turn of events. Especially not when none of the other people in the kitchen seemed shocked by the sight of me wearing his vest.

"Shit, sorry." He lifted his hands in a gesture of surrender. "I heard you brought the chick from the judge's office back to the clubhouse, but I missed out on the fact that you claimed her. I assumed you were just worried about her tipping him off to the fact that we're onto him before we got what we needed."

Cat rolled her eyes as she moved bacon from the frying pan to the paper-towel-lined plate. "If you didn't figure that out on your own, you were right about not being as observant as usual. Maybe you've been spending too much time at your keyboard lately."

"Or maybe I'm just having fun pushing his buttons," Grey suggested with a grin.

"Leave Doc alone," Scout muttered, flinging his arm around Cat's shoulders and pulling her against his side. "He's finally less of a grump now that he's caught himself some sunshine."

"And earned you fifty bucks," Cat mumbled.

Leaning close to Kendrick, I whispered, "What's she talking about?"

"Nothing important, baby." He glowered at the couple, who were both grinning at us. "They just like to make silly bets with each other to keep things interesting."

I was certain there was more to the story but judging by the way he was glaring at them, I probably didn't want to know. Instead of asking, I gave into my hunger and dug into the stack of pancakes after slathering them with syrup. But I made a mental note to ask Cat about it later.

11

DOC

I should never have brought her out of our room without my cut. I had no fucking clue what I was thinking. While Oakley ate, I shot off a quick text to Mac. When it became apparent that the men of the Silver Saints fell fast and hard, our prez had a stash of "property of" vests made so that when we needed one, rather than taking weeks to order it, we only needed to have the names added as long as he had the right size. Hopefully, I'd have my property patch on Oakley by Monday.

Grey took his plate to the sink, and on his way out of the room, he sent a pointed glance at Snowball who was sleeping in my lap. "Heard you were pussy-whipped," he murmured with a grin.

"If you don't want to lose your teeth, then shut the fuck up and get lost," I growled. He just burst out laughing as he walked to the door. Before he got too far, I had a thought and shouted, "Spread the word. Off-limits!"

Grey waved a hand in acknowledgment then disappeared.

I turned back to my woman who was just finishing up, and she giggled. "I guess I see what you meant this morning."

"About what, baby?" I asked casually, enjoying the way she laughed and smiled.

"About jealousy being hot."

That got my full attention. "Is that so?"

She nodded almost shyly, which made me smile because she certainly hadn't been shy the night before.

"Guess I better take advantage," I grunted as I got to my feet, dumping Snowball on the chair I'd been using. The little ball of fluff could wait down here with Cat and Scout while we were busy in bed. Then I bent over and scooped Oakley into my arms, heading straight for the stairs.

When we reached the top, I couldn't hold back any longer and kissed her sweet mouth as I made my way to our room. At the door, I reluctantly ripped my mouth away from hers and set her on her feet. After opening it, I put light pressure on her stomach to back her into the room, then slammed the door shut behind me.

My mouth was on hers immediately, and by the time we'd stumbled to the bed, our clothes were gone. I lifted Oakley, and her legs locked around my waist so that we fell onto the mattress together.

Suddenly, I saw a flash of white fluff in my peripheral vision before I felt the slight movement of Snowball landing on the mattress. I'd been so absorbed in kissing Oakley that I hadn't realized he'd followed us up here.

I turned my head, and he was practically glaring at me as if insulted that he hadn't been invited to the fun. I gave him an even more ferocious scowl, and after a second, he backed up and jumped off the bed, running over to disappear into his crate.

Oakley giggled, and the corners of my mouth kicked up at the sound. I fucking loved it when she smiled or laughed...or did anything at all. I loved everything about her. I wanted to tell her, but I didn't think she was ready. To keep myself from blurting it out, I slid down her body and devoured her pussy. After driving her to a quick orgasm, I climbed back up and stopped to hover over her stomach, bending down to place a soft kiss on her belly.

Once I was covering her from head to toe, I stared into her eyes as I said, "If you aren't already pregnant, gonna fix that right now."

Excitement flared in Oakley's eyes, and I grinned. "Like the sound of that, don't you, baby? You want my fat cock filling you with come until you're carrying my baby?"

Oakley bit her lip, still a little unsure, despite the longing in her eyes. It was clear that she hadn't really thought about whether it was something she wanted or not.

"Always gonna take care of you, baby. And that means making sure all of your dreams come true."

The last of the hesitancy clouding her features cleared away, and her brown orbs glinted with hope.

Desire burned in my gut, and my control was razor thin. Keeping eye contact, I slowly slid inside her, carefully because her tight pussy was still getting used to my girth. Oakley's eyes rolled to the back of her head, and her back arched, thrusting her tits up. "Look at me, baby," I commanded. I waited for her head to lift, then I sucked one of her distended peaks into my mouth as I retreated and thrust back in.

Once again, she looked away, and I growled, "Eyes on me, Oakley."

She blinked a few times before locking gazes with me.

I pulled back and thrust in, going impossibly deep this time, bumping into her cervix. I nearly lost control right then, knowing I'd be shooting my load right into her unprotected womb. But I managed to hold off, determined to make her come before me.

My hands traveled all over her silky skin as I ate at her mouth. Then I dragged my tongue down to her tits and loved on them until she was writhing with desperate need.

"Kendrick, please," she whimpered.

"Fuck," I groaned when her pussy convulsed around my shaft, sucking me deep inside her. "Come, baby."

Oakley screamed my name as her climax crashed into her, and it milked the last bit of my control from me.

"Oakley," I grunted before I exploded. "Fuck!"

When our breathing and heart rates began to normalize, I withdrew, chuckling at her adorable mewl of protest. Then I rolled to my side and turned her over, pulling her back against my front, then entered her again. For the moment, I was content just to hold her while buried deep inside her.

After a few minutes, Oakley asked a question about my family. We spent the next hour getting to know each other a little better. Eventually though, just holding her wasn't enough, and I began to move, slowly rocking against her ass. She moaned and pressed herself back, meeting each thrust. I took her lazily, making love to her, something I'd never expected to be capable of. But Oakley brought out another side of me. She was my everything now. She came before everything and everyone...even the brotherhood, which was something I never thought I'd say.

While she was taking a nap, I dressed and stepped into the hall to make some calls. I needed to get the ball rolling on moving into my house. The rooms at the clubhouse were decently soundproofed, but just the thought of anyone hearing her sounds of pleasure made me feel homicidal. And the bathroom thing...I'd escorted her to it earlier, stood guard until she was finished and took her back to our room.

The house would be cleaned up and ready for furniture delivery the following week. I'd set up accounts with several places so she could order whatever she wanted, and she'd have my credit card for anything else. Now I just had to tie her even closer to me so she wouldn't question moving in with me so quickly—even faster than a lot of my club brothers. But no way in hell was I going to spend my nights apart from my woman now that I'd found her...and done my best to make sure she was carrying my baby.

I owed past me a pat on the back for getting ahead on schoolwork because not having to worry about writing the five-page paper that I needed to turn in on Wednesday meant that I got to enjoy my weekend with Kendrick. We spent a fair amount of that time in bed, much to Snowball's disgust. Luckily, my spoiled ball of fluff took a liking to Scout and Cat, so he was happy to hang out in their room when we needed a little privacy.

Unfortunately, we couldn't stay cuddled up in bed together today. Not when I had classes and Kendrick had some kind of run he needed to do for the club. One he couldn't give me any details about because it was club business. I had a feeling I'd hear that phrase more often than I would appreciate.

"I don't like the idea of you going to campus while I'm out of town," he grumbled, pulling me against his chest after we both finished getting ready for our day.

I patted his broad chest. "Nobody saw you at the courthouse, and the security guard told me to have a good night when I left. There's no reason for the judge to think that you're looking into him yet, and nothing to connect us even if he was suspicious. But if I miss my classes, there's a chance that would raise a red flag because I never skip. I won the perfect attendance award all four years in high school, and I would've gotten the same every semester since I got to college if they had them there too."

Kendrick didn't look impressed by my logic. "Your safety is a fuck of a lot more important than a perfect attendance record nobody is even keeping track of."

"Why am I not surprised you ignored the entire first half of what I just said?" I shook my head with a sigh. "Would it make you feel better if someone came with me to school? They wouldn't be able to come into the lecture hall with me, but they can keep an eye out while they wait outside."

He flashed me a cocky grin. "I already have a prospect who's going to be on you. Carter has been instructed to take you to campus and make sure you're safe."

"Okay, then you don't have anything to worry about." I jerked my chin toward the door. "So get going. The sooner you leave for your run, the sooner you'll get back to me."

He kissed me breathless before whispering, "Be good, baby."

I watched him walk out the door, wondering how I could follow through with my plan while a prospect was watching me.

"I'm not sure how Doc missed it, but I sure didn't."

I'd been so focused on Kendrick, that I hadn't realized anyone else had come into the large space where everyone hung out. "Missed what?"

"How disappointed you looked when he said he put Carter on you." Cat strolled over and bumped her hip against mine.

"Now that you mention it, I noticed the same thing." Harlowe's brows drew together as she turned to look at me. She was Link's wife, and I'd just met her this morning at breakfast. Her husband was the club's treasurer, and she'd been on the back of his bike when he'd come to the clubhouse to get some work done while their kids were at school.

My mind blanked under their scrutiny. "I...um..."

"Oooh, now I really want to know what's up." Harlowe rubbed her palms together with a grin. "Whatever she wants to get up to has to be good if she's that nervous about a prospect keeping eyes on her."

I heaved a deep sigh and scanned the room to make sure we were still alone. "Okay, so this is probably going to sound like an awful idea to you two, but I was thinking I could pop into the office to see if I could find something that would help Kendrick with the judge."

"The judge?" Harlowe asked.

I explained how I came to meet Kendrick while he was breaking into the judge's office. "I'm worried that he used up all of his luck on Friday night. If Judge Timkins is crooked and he gets caught next time, they'll throw him in jail for years."

Cat tapped her finger against her chin. "You've had your internship there for a while already?"

I nodded. "Yeah, I started two months ago."

"And you're in the biometrics system?" Harlowe asked.

"Uh-huh," I confirmed.

"With access codes and everything?" Cat wanted to know.

"Yup."

The two women turned to look at each other, grinning widely.

My eyes widened as the implication of their friendly grilling and smiles hit me. "Wait...do you *not* think it's an awful idea? Even though the thing with the judge is club business, and Doc wants me to stay out of it?"

Harlowe got serious as she explained, "Normally, I would never urge one of the women to stick their nose into club business, but it sounds as though you're kind of already in the middle of it since you work in the judge's office."

"When you really think about it, all you're planning to do is pop into the office, where people expect you to be anyway," Cat added. "And if you go when the judge is in court, you won't even run into him."

Harlowe pursed her lips. "But you said that the judge keeps his door locked when he's not in his office, so how will you get in there without anyone noticing?"

"Miss Stuchy keeps a key in her top desk drawer." I thought about it for a minute. "If someone could create a distraction and get her into the hallway for a little bit, I could grab the key and sneak into the judge's office to give it a quick check."

"How long would you need us to keep your boss busy?" Cat asked.

I pressed my lips together while I thought about the most likely hiding spots in Judge Timkins' office. "Kendrick was near the wall behind the judge's desk instead of over by the filing cabinets. Which would not be the best place to hide anything since he's had me do some filing in them. If there's a hidden safe or something like that, I will probably not be able to find it. But I should be able to search the desk in like...five minutes."

They grinned at each other again before turning back to me with a nod. Then Cat said, "We can keep her distracted for that long."

My eyes widened. "You guys want to come to the courthouse with me?"

"Yup." Harlowe's smile widened. "That's the beauty of this plan. You'll never really be alone, so that should help soothe the wild beast when Kendrick finds out what you did."

"If anyone asks, you can say that you forgot something in the office when you went in to make copies on Friday night, and you decided to stop by to pick it up while you were out with us since we were already downtown." Cat waved her hand between the three of us. "While we're waiting in the hallway for you, we'll get into a loud disagreement. Your boss won't be able to stop herself from coming to see what all the ruckus is about, and that'll be your chance."

Her plan sounded better than anything I'd come up with. "What about the prospect that's supposed to take me to campus?"

"I'm the treasurer's old lady"—Harlowe jerked her thumb at Cat—"and she belongs to the VP. Poor Carter isn't going to question what we say."

"Poor Carter." Cat gave me a sheepish grin. "He's the sacrificial lamb on our outing. After we talk him into taking us to the courthouse, he's going to be in deep shit with Doc."

I bit my bottom lip and nodded. "Yeah, I hate that he's going to get in trouble, but do you see any other way around it? I was hoping Kendrick would tell me that I'd be fine on campus when I suggested he send someone with me. I wasn't expecting him to tell me that he'd already set it up."

"Because you've only been with Doc for a weekend." Cat patted me on the back. "You'll soon learn that if you give our guys an inch, they'll take a mile."

Harlowe nodded with a laugh. "And they'll do the same even when you don't give them an inch."

"But they sure do make their bossiness worth the while," Cat added with a wink.

Harlowe wagged her brows. "Their punishments, too. Which is why you can count me in on this. It's been a while since I've earned myself a spanking."

I really hoped my search of the judge's desk yielded something that Kendrick could use...and maybe even earned myself a spanking, too. Because the spark in Harlowe's eyes when she talked about Link spanking her made me curious as heck about how it would feel if Kendrick did the same to me.

13

DOC

I'd been pissed as fuck to be assigned a run that morning. I wasn't comfortable leaving Oakley's safety to anyone, especially not when she was in the middle of the mess with Timkins.

But this pickup had been to one of my contacts, and they would only give the shit to me, so Mac ordered Knight, Grey, and me to go on the short run. We'd only been gone a few hours, but I was still anxious as fuck on our way back. I'd been tempted to keep Oakley locked up in the compound, but I'd promised to support her dreams, and I wouldn't go back on my word. If she needed to be on campus, then I had to suck it up and let her go.

I'd been in backwoods territory, and my cell service had been spotty, so the text from Carter didn't come through until I was an hour out from Silver Saints' territory.

Carter: Need to come to the courthouse asap.

Fuck. That couldn't be anything good. I waved to Knight, and we pulled over to the side of the road.

"I gotta get downtown. Carter texted. Problem at the courthouse."

Grey raised an eyebrow. "Isn't Carter watching your woman?"

I nodded, my brow furrowed and my mouth turned down in a deep frown. "Going to kill that motherfucker," I growled, my trigger finger itching at the thought.

"I'll take the package back to Mac," Grey offered. "You go handle your woman."

Knight nodded. "I'll come downtown with you. Just in case shit hits the fan since that seems par for the course whenever one of you falls for a woman."

I lifted my chin, then kicked up my stand and took off with Knight on my tail.

We drove like bats outta hell, and as we were approaching the courthouse, I spotted Carter, Cat, Harlowe, and Oakley coming out the side entrance, the one I'd broken into just a few nights before.

The girls looked smug, and Carter looked worried. *Damn straight, he should be fucking terrified.*

Knight and I pulled our hogs into the closest parking spot, and Oakley glanced over at us since our bikes weren't exactly stealthy. Her expression turned guilty, and when I pulled off my helmet, she took a step back. I would've been worried she actually thought I'd hurt her, but there was no real fear in her eyes, just the knowledge that she was in deep shit.

I hopped off my ride, but before I could take a step, Knight's hand on my arm had me spinning around to put a fist in his face.

He ducked, and I missed, giving him a chance to snap, "Chill out, Doc. Just wanted to remind you where we are. You wanna kick the prospect's ass? It's your right, but you need to wait until we get back to the compound."

I bit back a roar of frustration and rage. As hard as it was to control myself, he was right.

Harlowe huffed and put her hands on her hips, and she turned an accusing glare on Carter. "You tattled?"

As I stalked up to them, I snarled, "It's the only reason he'll still be breathing tomorrow. Just might be through a tube."

Carter put his hands up in a gesture of surrender. "Sent the message as soon as I realized they wouldn't back down and would go with or without me. Wasn't going to touch a brother's old lady, so I did the next best thing. Let you know and went with them for protection."

What he said made sense, and after I had a chance to cool down, it might save him from ending up in the hospital. But at that moment, I couldn't see past the fact that my woman had been in a dangerous situation under his watch.

"You bring an SUV?" Knight asked Carter while I breathed deep and tried to get myself under control.

Carter nodded.

Knight jerked his thumb toward the parking lot. "Get your asses to the car," he growled. Then he pointed at Cat and Harlowe. "Talkin' to you two. Now."

It looked like the girls wanted to argue, but they knew better than to step between a patch and his property. Their old men would tan their hides for interfering—they were probably in for a punishment for helping Oakley in the first place. Which made me feel only slightly better.

I waited until Knight had guided the others away

before finally facing my woman. Her chin was lifted to a stubborn angle, and if I hadn't been so angry and still a little scared from what could have happened, I might have smiled.

"You," I grated through clenched teeth. "What happened to going to school?"

"This was more important," she said, her chin lifting another notch.

"More important than your perfect attendance record?" I drawled, giving myself another minute to calm down before we talked about what just happened.

"Yes. They don't keep attendance anyway. I–"

I'd heard enough. "You disobeyed me," I accused.

"Um." She shifted uncomfortably but didn't look away, which I highly respected. "You said I couldn't come to work, you didn't tell me I couldn't stop by to get something."

"Bullshit, baby. You knew exactly what I meant."

"I only stopped by to pick something up. I swear. I was in and out in less than ten minutes."

I crossed my arms over my chest and continued to glare at her. "Pick up what?"

She smiled and held out her hand, showing me a thick folder and a manila envelope. "Everything you need to have the judge arrested and put away."

I barely glanced at the items, more concerned with her lack of self-preservation. "You got any idea how much danger you put yourself in, Oakley?"

Her smile faded. "Seriously, Kendrick. Nobody even noticed me. And...don't you care that I got what you need?"

I closed the distance between us and curled an arm around her waist, then grabbed her chin with my free hand. "You are what I need," I rasped. "You and our baby."

Her mouth formed a little O, and I raised an eyebrow, emphasizing my subtle hint. She clearly hadn't thought about the fact that if she was pregnant, she'd put our child at risk too.

She sighed. "Okay, I wasn't thinking completely rationally. But you have the evidence now."

"I don't give a damn about the evidence, baby. Not when getting to it put the woman I love at risk."

"You love me?" I blinked up at Kendrick, pressing trembling fingers against my lips as my heart started to race.

He pulled me closer, threading his fingers through the back of my hair. "Damn straight, I do."

His answer sparked a flutter in my belly, but I was still having a hard time wrapping my head around the idea that this amazing man had fallen in love with me so quickly. "This isn't just a heat of the moment thing? Because I put myself out there to get you what you needed? And you think I might be carrying your baby after this past weekend?"

"I can see why you want to become a lawyer, baby. You're gonna be great at grilling people when they're on the stand." He brushed his lips against mine in a quick kiss. "But you've got this all wrong. I've seen many of my club brothers fall hard and fast for their women, but I never thought it would happen to me until I met you."

"Really?" I gasped, those flutters in my belly turning into full-on butterflies that had taken flight and were flapping their wings as hard as possible.

"I wouldn't have had Cat put you in my room if I didn't already know I was going to claim you." He captured my mouth in a deeper kiss that left me breathless and gripping his shoulders to hold myself steady. "Seems as though you're the only one who didn't realize what I was planning. I was acting so damn out of character, all it took was five seconds for Mac to figure out why and call me on my shit."

I smoothed my hands down his chest, tracing my fingers over the Silver Saints emblem on his vest. "I was so worried that you were going to get in trouble with how angry he seemed."

"Oh, he was still pissed as fuck because someone could've realized that I took you and clued the judge into the fact that the Silver Saints were looking into him." He chuckled and shook his head, flashing me a cocky grin. "But he couldn't say shit because he kidnapped Bridget out of her room on another MC's compound where her dad was the president."

"I really do need to ask her to tell me the story about how she and Mac got together," I muttered. "The things I've heard so far are pretty wild."

He quirked a brow. "Wilder than how we met?"

"Nah," I giggled.

His hold on my hair tightened as he peered down at me. "Then maybe your curiosity about my prez and his old lady can wait until after you tell me how you feel about me."

My smile was wide as I confessed, "I fell just as quickly."

"Is that your way of saying that you love me, baby?" he asked, the corners of his eyes crinkling as he returned my grin.

"Yes, I love you, too." I twined my arms around his neck and went up on my toes to press my lips against his. "So, so much."

"Thank fuck, baby." He dropped his forehead against mine. "Or else I would've had to kidnap you for real until you fell for me."

"From the little I've been told so far, I think Bridget already proved that you can't kidnap the willing," I teased, my heart full of happiness.

"Not sure how willing you should be since I'm pissed that you put yourself at risk. I would've come back to grab these from the judge's hiding place under the floor beneath his desk if the search of his house didn't turn up anything. Which I'm assuming would be the case since it looks like he was keeping the records for his dirty shit here."

"Oh." My shoulders slumped. "You already found where he kept this stuff?"

He lifted his head and nodded. "Yeah, on Friday night right as you walked into the office and interrupted my search."

Blown away by his explanation, I gaped at him. "Why didn't you just grab the stuff while I was making copies?"

"Because there was no way for me to be certain this was what he was keeping down there until I had the chance to check it out." He shook the file I'd given him. "And I didn't want to let you out of my sight in case shit hit the fan and I needed to get you outta the building fast. After years of putting the needs of the Silver Saints ahead of everything, your safety came first. Luckily, it's not a decision anyone's going to give me shit over because every other man who wears this cut would've done the same for their woman."

The television shows had definitely gotten a lot wrong about motorcycle clubs, and I couldn't be happier that Kendrick was the kind of man who wouldn't put me second. "If you'd told me that you were that close to grabbing this stuff, I would've stuck close to you while you searched the judge's hiding spot. Then you wouldn't have needed to worry about finding what you needed."

"I think it's safe to say that I don't live up to my reputation for being calm and collected when it comes to you," he admitted with a rueful grin. "But I wasn't worried, baby. Meeting you might've thrown me off my game a little on Friday night, but I didn't have any doubt that I'd be able to dig up whatever the judge was hiding. I'm the club's fixer because I'm damn good at ferreting out information and won't stop until I find what we need to keep my club brothers safe and outta jail."

I beamed a smile at him. "We really are the perfect fit. Once I graduate from law school and pass the bar, you can help me dig up information to help my clients, and I can help you keep the Silver Saints out of prison."

"Consider it a deal, baby." He captured my mouth in a deep kiss, his tongue tangling with mine until I was breathless...and had decided that we should seal every deal the same way. "The club could use a skilled attorney who's part of the family. We have two we use now, but one's too crooked to trust, and the other is too straight to get his hands dirty when we need it."

I winked at him. "Kinda like Goldilocks, I'll be just right."

"Because you're fucking perfect." He released the hair at the back of my head to brush my bangs away from my glasses. "Did your apartment come furnished?"

I shook my head, wondering if the abrupt change of topic was because he was going to suggest that he move in. We couldn't stay at the clubhouse forever, and now that I knew Kendrick loved me, I didn't see any reason we should be apart from each other. Especially not with how hectic my schedule was and how unpredictable his was. "No, everything in there is mine."

"Good, we can have the guys move all your shit to my house," he announced with a smirk. "Your stuff will be enough for us to start staying there. I bought it a few years ago, but it needed a fuck ton of work. Got most of it done, though. So there's no reason we can't move in. It's not too far from the clubhouse, so the drive to campus won't be bad."

My brows drew together. "You have a house?"

"No, *we* have a house," he corrected. "But you're gonna be the one who turns it into a home. I've let the place sit empty while I've fixed it up because shopping for furniture and shit is the last thing I want to do."

"I love shopping," I breathed, thinking about how much fun I'd have decorating a home for us.

"More proof that you're fucking perfect for me, sweet baby."

EPILOGUE

DOC

"**O**akley Lawson," I growled. "Get your ass over here."

My wife froze mid-tiptoe into the clubhouse kitchen. She looked uncertain and glanced at the door, clearly trying to decide whether to make a run for it.

"Don't even think about it, or your ass will be smarting every time you sit tomorrow."

I nearly rolled my eyes when she continued to contemplate. My girl had a naughty side that I adored. Although, it made it difficult to dole out spankings as a punishment when it made her wet.

Fuck. This train of thought was just turning me on. "You know I'll come up with a way for you to regret it."

Finally, she sighed and straightened, turning to face me. "Cat made cookies. I could smell them all the way up in our room." She rubbed her protruding belly and sniffed again before licking her lips.

I had one fucking rule for coming to the clubhouse with me. "What's the rule, baby?"

Her expression turned sheepish, and her cheeks heated. "None of the 'approved' escorts were available." She wrinkled her nose in irritation, and I bit back a smile. She was adorable when she was annoyed. When she was pissed, though, she was a hot fucking goddess.

"The rule, Oakley."

She sighed. "No wandering anywhere alone."

Since she'd gotten too big to wear her property vest, I'd forbade her from being at the clubhouse unless I was by her side the entire time. But she was a few days past her due date and more emotional than usual, plus I didn't want to be away from her in case she went into labor. So I'd agreed to bring her with me when I went to meet with my officers to discuss another problem that needed my attention.

"I wasn't really alone, though..." She trailed off as she looked around the floor and frowned. When her eyes came back to me, she finally noticed that Snowball was in my arms. She gasped dramatically and hissed, "Traitor."

I tried not to laugh at her indignant expression, but it was cute as hell. Shaking my head, I walked toward her and transferred Snowball to her so I could put my arm around her shoulders. "You'll be grumpy as fuck if I don't let you have some cookies, but then you're gonna lie down and rest."

"But--"

"No buts, baby."

Oakley yawned, and I smirked. "Don't be so smug," she muttered.

"If you aren't tired enough to nap, there are ways I can help you with that," I teased with a wicked grin.

Oakley's cheeks turned pink, and she squeezed her legs together. "Um, I don't think I'm hungry for cookies anymore..."

"I CHANGED MY MIND. I want cookies. Can we go home and get some?" Oakley panted after a small contraction.

I rolled my eyes and leaned over the hospital bed to give my woman a hard kiss. "You're about to have our daughter, babe, and you're thinking about cookies?"

She frowned and huffed. "They said it would be a few hours."

I'd taken Oakley's mind off the cookies when I ate her for a snack earlier. Apparently, what they said about sex making you go into labor wasn't just an old wives' tale. Not long after she climaxed, her water broke, and we headed to the hospital. When the doctor told her she wasn't ready to deliver right then, she'd started coming up with reasons to leave and return later.

I would have thought cookies were her latest excuse, except she was licking her lips and staring dreamily off into space. Another contraction hit, and she breathed through it, then munched on an ice chip and stared at me stubbornly. "Do you love me or not?"

My brow rose. "More than anything. But if you expect me to prove it by breaking you outta here, you can forget it, baby."

"I neeeeeed cookies, Kendrick!"

Pulling out my cell, I shot off a quick text. "Okay, baby. Relax. I'll get you some cookies."

"That last time you gave me anything, I ended up in the hospital about to push a watermelon through a hole the size of a grapefruit!" She grabbed her stomach and groaned as another contraction hit. "We are never having sex again."

I snorted at her ridiculous statement. My wife loved my cock, and we both knew she couldn't go very long without it. Not that I was any less addicted to her pussy.

Oakley glared at me, and I put a straight face on. "Whatever you want, baby."

Ten minutes later, I breathed a sigh of relief when Oakley stopped crushing my hand and clapped excitedly as Cat strolled into the room carrying a container of cookies.

But before my wife could take one bite, her doctor came in to check her progress, then announced it was time for her to deliver.

Oakley refused until she could eat at least one cookie. The doctor looked at me, probably expecting me to help since she wasn't supposed to eat anything at this point, but I wasn't stupid enough to get between my pregnant woman and her sweets.

"NEXT TIME I knock you up, you can't have any sugar," I murmured as I stared down at my perfect baby girl.

"What?" Oakley shot me a confused glance.

"You made her too sweet. I'm gonna have to buy more shotguns."

EPILOGUE
OAKLEY

Attending law school was difficult for anyone but doing it while having babies and being married to a hot biker was even harder. There were times when I was going on only a couple of hours of sleep and had an exam that I questioned if I could turn my dream of becoming a lawyer into reality. But my husband and our Silver Saints family were with me every step of the way.

Kendrick changed more diapers than I did and handled just as many middle-of-the-night feedings. The other old ladies babysat whenever I had class, and he had to go on a run. And the day had finally come when we'd find out if all of their support had paid off.

Rolling my chair away from the desk in the room

I claimed as my home office, I called, "Kendrick, the state bar just posted that exam results have been released."

He knew how nervous I'd been about passing the bar, so he moved quickly to get to my side. I rubbed the back of my neck as I listened to the stomp of his feet as he raced through the house. When he reached the door, he beamed me a reassuring smile. "I have no doubt that you've got this, baby. You studied your ass off for the exam, and you're smart as fuck. I'm willing to bet you passed it with flying colors."

"A bet, huh?" I grinned up at him as he pressed his hands on the arms of my chair, towering over me. "What would you want if you win?"

"Quit trying to distract me." He chuckled and shook his head. "I know you're nervous about your score, but we both know you're gonna give me whatever I want when we celebrate you officially becoming a lawyer."

I wagged my brows. "Are you gonna punish me if I didn't pass?"

After our little foray to the courthouse back when Kendrick and I first got together, I'd learned why Harlowe had been looking forward to getting spanked by Link. Although I had found the information the Silver Saints needed on the judge, Kendrick had still been mad—and scared—enough to insist that I'd earned myself a punishment. Only it had backfired on him because I'd enjoyed the heck out of the feel of his hand on my butt, and my getting turned on had led to him losing control and putting the hard-on he'd gotten from spanking me to good use. So it was fair to say that I'd gone out of my way to find reasons for him to spank me over the past five or so years.

Kendrick had been more than happy to play along...until now. His dark eyes were serious as he crouched between my legs, lacing his fingers through mine. "Sorry, baby. Not this time. If that score isn't what you're hoping for, I know it's gonna mess with your head. I'll fuck you to as many orgasms as you want and test you with those flashcards you made as many times as it takes for you to be ready the next time you can take it. But I'm not gonna punish you for trying your hardest to achieve the dream you've worked so long for. Especially not when you told me how many law school grads won't pass their first time. We've got time, baby. There's no rush. If you don't make the cut this time, you can chill with the kids and me while you prep for the next one."

My eyes filled with tears, and I sniffled. "I don't understand how anyone could have ever thought you were grumpy when you're the sweetest man in the whole wide world."

"Only because you bring it out of me with all of your sunshine," he insisted, pausing in getting back to his feet to brush his lips against mine. "You and the kids get this side of me while everyone else gets the grump."

I stroked my palm over his bearded cheek. "The grump who'd do whatever it takes to keep everyone he cares about safe."

Stepping back, he swiveled my chair so I was facing the computer. "And it's time to find out if you're gonna be able to help me with that mission now or if we'll have to wait six months before you can take the test again and take over for Jasper and that bastard, Finch."

His absolute faith in me soothed my nerves. So did the reminder that I didn't have to worry about getting hired by a law firm like my peers. I had a ready-made client who'd more than keep me on my toes between all the businesses the Silver Saints owned and the kind of trouble they found themselves in every time one of the single men fell for someone. And beyond that, the family I'd built with Kendrick meant everything to me. If it took another six months for me to pass the bar, then I'd just enjoy the heck out of my extra time with our children.

But as I pulled up my state bar applicant portal and squeezed my eyes shut as the exam results loaded, the loud whoop Kendrick let out told me that I'd been worried for nothing. I'd achieved my lifelong dream of becoming a lawyer...and had my celebration with my husband to look forward to that night.

Curious about Knight, and Cash? Their stories are up next!

Did you miss Mac & Bridget's story? Or Link & Harlowe's? You can grab both of them plus one more in Silver Saints MC: Volume 1!

If you sign up for our newsletter, you'll get an email from us with a link to claim a free copy of The Virgin's Guardian, which is no longer available to purchase.

ABOUT THE AUTHOR

The writing duo of Elle Christensen and Rochelle Paige team up under the Fiona Davenport pen name to bring you sexy, insta-love stories filled with alpha males. If you want a quick & dirty read with a guaranteed happily ever after, then give Fiona Davenport a try!

Don't miss out on new release news and giveaways; sign up for our newsletter!

Printed in Dunstable, United Kingdom